AGAINST ALL ODDS

A Basketball Story

by

Drew Oakley

RoseDog Books
PITTSBURGH, PENNSYLVANIA 15238

RoseDog Books
585 Alpha Drive
Suite 103
Pittsburgh, PA 15238
Visit our website at *www.rosedogbookstore.com*

ISBN: 978-1-4809-7024-3
eISBN: 978-1-4809-7001-4

CHAPTER 1

"Huddle up! Move your butts! Twenty seconds left and we're down one!" Coach Chris wipes moisture from his forehead to keep it from dripping into and stinging his flared eyes, eyes as determined as a bull seeing red.

"Get the ball to, Jamal!"

Coach and I both look to Jamal, and I'm sure we are thinking the same thing: *Jamal can save this game. I know it!*

"Jamal, just do your thing!" Coach cups his hands over his mouth so Jamal can hear him.

The coach's reassurance widens Jamal's smile.

"I got this, Coach. I was born ready."

With the state championship for Massachusetts the prize, Jamal, the high school junior already named National Player of the Year by ESPN, knows college scouts are in the bleachers. Coach "K" from Duke and Roy Williams from North Carolina had already called to talk.

I'm watching and sweating like a bear ready to pounce on dinner. *If he gets this basket, he's got his ticket to play for any school he wants. It is not too big a fish for Jamal. It sort of seems like nothing is out of Jamal's reach now.*

When Jamal said he was born ready, he meant it, and Coach Chris knows it. Rumor has it Jamal was born with a basketball in his hands. He was eleven pounds at birth and walking by ten months.

1

By three, he could read and do basic math. The kid seems destined for greatness.

He is a child prodigy in other ways, too, which gives people the expectation he will play Division 1 basketball and eventually be the number-one pick in the NBA draft when it is time. At six feet, two inches, and two hundred twenty pounds in his junior year of high school, Jamal has the dribbling talent of Allen Iverson, shoots like Steph Curry and dunks like a young Vince Carter, is as crafty a scorer as Paul Pierce, and passes like Magic Johnson.

I can feel the vibrations in the gym doing drumbeats on my heart. Even the floor quakes. I look up and see Mia, Jamal's and my best friend, screaming off the Richter scale, her face a strange shade of red I haven't seen since kindergarten, when someone spilled her milk and took her cookie.

The whistle blows and the teams take to the court. I am sitting on the back of the bench, more like a water boy than a playing team member. Coach says I work hard at playing ball, but I'm too small, so I can be a benchwarmer. Looking around, the room dazzles with colors from the fans holding up signs rooting for their teams. I see Jamal zoned in and ready to do what he was born to do.

I have been Jamal's best friend since kindergarten and technically his brother since the third grade, when his parents just left one day. Theirs was a poor family that could not support itself, and Jamal was the one bright spot. They didn't want to ruin it for him.

The note they left Jamal simply said:

We cannot take care of you, son. Stay with Kevin's family. They will help you get to a better place than we could.

We will love you forever.

Jamal didn't know where his parents went or what happened to them. The note told of their disgrace that they could not help this talented kid through life. My folks took him in.

I mean, I get it, and I felt sorry for him, too. But why did my family have to take him in?

During the first week he lived with us, Misty, our loyal fifty-five-pound Norwegian elkhound, fell in love with Jamal. After a month I understood why. Jamal didn't feel sorry for himself—or didn't let anyone know if he did. His family may have been poor, but they protected his ego while he was growing up so he could stay on top of his life.

We became best buddies. His personality made him easy to be with, and he was so kind. Sometimes I resented that his natural helpfulness showed me up. So I learned by imitating him.

The ref gives the ball to Brian, the starting small forward, to inbound. Everyone knows that Jamal is getting the ball. The person covering him is his biggest instate rival, Curtis Winters, who was ranked third in the country.

I can hear Curtis trash-talking Jamal. Jamal never talks trash; his play does his talking.

I hear Curtis say, "Ay, Jamal, what's up? Thought you were number one in the country.

It's my time now. You ain't got nothin' on me, boy, no way you're scorin'."

Then for the first time, I hear Jamal talk back. "Yo, man, shut up or I'm going to embarrass your sorry self."

"Oh, yeah, just try to, man. Just try to," Curtis taunts.

Jamal looks right at Curtis. "You really should not have pissed me off."

Curtis keeps trash-talking and seems ready to shove Jamal, but Jamal says nothing back and gets the ball from the inbound. I've never seen Jamal mad at someone before, and I know he is going to win the game no matter how good the defense plays against him.

Jamal goes to the center of the court near where Curtis is playing tight defense, still lunging at Jamal.

Jamal and I always practice game winners when we are hanging out, and he has developed so many ways to hit one, it's not even funny. With fifteen seconds left, Jamal starts dribbling to his right, crosses over left, and then goes behind his back, followed by a step-back dribble.

Curtis falls to the ground, stopping his fall with his hands. Everyone is yelling for him to shoot, but Jamal's not shooting, and I am thinking, *What is he doing?*

Instead of hitting the open jump shot, Jamal yells, "Yo, get up!"

Curtis, pissed off, gets up with nine seconds left on the clock.

He is right up and so close on Jamal you could say they were stuck together. Then Jamal does the unthinkable. It looks to me like everything is going in slow motion. He does a behind-the-back dribble, then sends the ball through Curtis's legs. Curtis has a look of disbelief on his face, and so does everyone else in the building. Jamal does a spin move around the center at the free-throw line and makes the game-winning layup just as time expires.

The scoreboard reads, "Beverly, 90, Roxbury, 89." It is a street-ball move in the state championship game. This play is going to be on Sports Center's "Top Ten" plays, for sure. I know Jamal's hype will increase from this, especially with pros and college coaches at the game.

I can only dream about being a basketball hero. Jamal actually is.

Fans swarm the court, most surrounding Jamal, but he leaves, walks right over to me, and picks me up. His tall, lanky body lifts me—skinny and giddy—as though I am a toy boy.

"We made it, Kev. We made it!"

He is so happy, and so am I. His smile goes from ear to ear.

Jamal screams, "Anything is possible!"

He puts me down, hugs me, and then some fans lift him on their shoulders and carry him away.

CHAPTER 2

"Jamal is in the hospital!"

Waking up to my mom screaming and crying is something I never want to do again. The light on my alarm clock flashes 2:00 A.M.

"He got in an accident, and he's hurt really bad. Get up, Kevin. We have to go to the hospital."

I had heard my folks talk about their "heartache" when Grandma died, but I never understood the word. How can your heart ache? Now I understand, except I feel it in my gut; it's like being punched in the stomach. Shutting my eyes, I hope to open them again when this would all be a nightmare and I would smell breakfast cooking downstairs.

No. When I open them again, I see Mom and Dad both in tears. I feel like passing out, but my parents keep me in the moment and make me get into the car to go to the hospital.

"Why was Jamal outside? I never heard him leave. It's cold outside; didn't he realize that?" I protest as if the angry words will protect Jamal.

"Jamal told me he was going to the court down the street to shoot baskets because he was still full of adrenaline from the game and couldn't sleep," Mom explained. "He didn't want to wake you up, so he went on his own and took Misty with him. When the police arrived, there was Misty, spread across his body and howling. They had to hold her back when the ambulance came. They found us off the address on her tags."

"W-w-what did the police say?" I ask.

"They think he was in the crosswalk, and you know, Jamal never walks against the light. It looks like a hit-and-run. There was only one witness 'cause it was so late, and she described the make and model of the car but didn't see the license plate." Dad, washed out, doesn't want to talk anymore.

Even though Jamal was adopted, he is just as much a part of the family as all of us. He tries his hardest at everything and to help whenever he can.

I stand there thinking about how he has been a once-in-a-lifetime person for me to know.

I never thought a person who had put in so much effort to succeed could have something like this happen to him.

We pull up to the hospital, and I am still trying to wake up from my nightmare and shaking with fear.

We are sent to the surgery waiting room. I sit down next to Mom and put my head in her lap as she rubs my head.

CHAPTER 3

"Kevin, wake up. Kev, c'mon." Mom is shaking me.

"Wow. I was having the worst nightmare."

"It's not a nightmare, Kevin."

It all rushes back to me like a tidal wave. I can't take a deep breath. I'm in a really unfamiliar place with the smell of disinfectant choking me. The ceiling lights flicker annoyingly, forcing me to squint to see well. I know I'm not home 'cause Mom would never let that happen to one of our lights at home.

"Where is Jamal? Is he okay? When can I see him?" I am screaming at my folks.

Dad, resigned to the situation, tells me,

"Slow down, son. When the doctor comes out to talk to us, we'll find out."

I get up to run through the surgery doors, but Dad grabs my shirt and pulls me back. I try to fight against him but he hugs me, which it turns out I really needed.

"Kev, he's alive!" Dad sighs.

I'm still trying to understand what might be happening inside that surgery door.

"I know, Dad. Thanks." For the hug, I should have told him, not his pep talk.

A police officer walks in and waits for us to notice him.

"Sorry to bother you all. I know this is a bad time, but I have some questions whenever you're ready."

"Sure," Dad says.

"Did Jamal have anyone mad at him? Anyone who might want to hurt him?" the officer asks.

The thought *Just one person* floats through my mind.

"We have a description of the vehicle but unfortunately, it is one of the most popular cars and colors."

"Like what?" Dad asks.

"A white Toyota Rav4. We'll keep an eye out for it and you should, too. If it's someone who knows Jamal, you might also see this car around. Keep your eyes open." The officer looks at each one of us. "Thanks for your help. Here is my information if you see or hear anything." The officer passes his business cards. "Sorry about your brother," he says to me, "and," he looks at my folks, "your son."

As soon as the officer leaves, the doctor comes through the surgery door and stops a few feet away. I'm guessing he's thinking about what he is going to tell us.

"Jamal is out of surgery, and he's doing as well as can be expected."

What does that mean? But I don't say it out loud. I know I'm in shock and not sure what will come out of my mouth if I try to talk.

"Right now, he is paralyzed from the waist down. He is not able to walk, but we can't tell if this is permanent or will change."

I hear a gasp and realize it came from me. "Can I see him?" I plead.

"No, son, not yet. He'll be in recovery for a couple more hours. The nurse will come get you when he's awake."

"What are his chances to walk again?"

I can see from the look on Mom's face she dreaded asking that question.

The surgeon eyes us sadly.

"We always hope for miracles, but there is only a ten-percent chance he'll walk in the first year. If he doesn't, his chances go down to one percent the following year."

I refuse to believe what I'm hearing. "He'll be fine and he'll be back on the court, I'm sure of it."

I am the only one sitting in the waiting room who believes this. I know this for a fact because my Mom says, "He might have to learn to play from a wheelchair. If anyone can do that, Jamal can."

The doctor shakes his head, and I look down so he cannot see the tears in my eyes.

Dad asks, "Does his injury have a name?"

"He has a lower spinal cord injury, which left him with paraplegia paralysis of just his legs," the surgeon replies.

Hearing a name for what Jamal has feels like a jolt of lightning, making his illness more real.

Two hours, three bags of Doritos, and an orange juice from the vending machine later, the nurse heads toward us.

"You may go in now. He's awake but groggy. He understands he can't walk but doesn't realize that this could be permanent. Please, don't stress any of that information to him now."

We follow the nurse. The closer I get to his room, the more in denial I become. I kind of feel like they have a person in there they *think* is Jamal.

Standing outside his room, my feet turn to lead. I can't walk in.

"Kev, you don't have to go in if you don't want to."

Mom puts her hand on my shoulder. My dad, though, takes my arm.

"You are probably the one person he wants to see the most. Let's go."

Relief runs through my body when I see Jamal has a smile on his face. I run over and give him a hug.

"I'm so happy to see you smiling. I was nervous to walk in here."

"I can still use my upper body. And I have you guys. What more could I ask from this situation?"

"We're going to make sure you have the best medical care." Dad's tone is very reassuring.

"Thanks, Mom and Dad," Jamal says.

I like to hear him call my folks "Mom" and "Dad," just like I do. He looks at me with a huge smile on his face, just like he had when he hit the game winner last night, which now feels like it was days ago.

"Yo, Kev, I've decided you're going to have to be the new star of the team until I'm up and back playing," Jamal says.

I can see he means it. Mom smiles and Dad shakes his head.

Jamal gets a disappointed look on his face. "No, Kev, I'm serious. You are going to be the star of the team until I come back to play myself!"

I kinda laugh at this, and Jamal gets angry for the first time.

"Yo, man, if you can't even have any faith in you being the star of the team, then how can I ever have any faith in walking again? The odds are against us, but we are going to do this."

The room goes silent for a minute, and no one knows what to say. Jamal breaks the silence.

"Man, we are both going to fight to do things no one says we can do. You're my brother and we're going to do this together. Every step of the way, I am going to have your back and you're going to have mine. We are not giving up on our dreams."

I know Jamal sees the tears in my eyes.

"I know you have always dreamed of being the star player, and no one puts in as much work as us, and that is not stopping now. The only thing different now is that my new dream is walking again. My basketball dreams might be gone, and I have to face that. But Kev, I am not letting you give up on yours. We are both going to be inspirations for each other, and we ARE going to get through this."

Mom and Dad and I are in shock at his pep talk. I am deeply touched and now motivated to not fail my brother.

"He needs rest now." The nurse motions for us to say our goodbyes and leave his room.

As we walk out, Jamal's smile leaves his face. I hug him. Two weeks before Christmas, and I have to leave him in the hospital.

"See you, sport." He smiles, closes his eyes, and is asleep before we leave the room.

CHAPTER 4

Wow, it is 12:30 at night and I still can't fall asleep. I have school in the morning, and I hate not getting enough sleep. But, who am I to be complaining about missing a few hours of sleep when my best friend cannot walk, go to school, chase his dreams, or even leave the hospital?

I need to start appreciating these things I take for granted and not get so mad or sad about all the small stuff. I am pathetic. I always complain or get stressed about stupid little things. Man, Jamal had his real parents walk out on him and now he may never walk again, and he still isn't complaining and is finding a way to deal with life.

Me, I'm supposed to become the star of the team? I mean, I am only one hundred and twenty-five pounds. I am a hard worker. I don't want to fail Jamal, and I really want this for me and for him. That's just like Jamal, to have that no-quit attitude and still care about my dreams and me even though his dreams might have just been destroyed. He is still looking out for me just like I would look out for him. I am going all out on this for him.

CHAPTER 5

A delicious smell from the kitchen is probably the only thing that could have woken me up and gotten me out of bed. Sitting at the kitchen table, I turn on the TV, my first mistake of the day, because ESPN, my favorite station, is breaking the story about Jamal's accident and his paralysis. They interview sports analysts and coaches who are saying how sad they are to learn about this tragedy happening to such a talented athletic. Across the screen flashes an alert that we should be on the lookout for a white Toyota Rav4 with possible front-end damage. The alert tells us to call the police with information, especially a license plate number.

"Do not approach the driver," the announcer continues.

Next is an interview with some players from the Boston Celtics.

"We will pay for any surgery Jamal needs," one says.

The sense of caring comes from everywhere. Even the local news station carries Jamal as the big story of the day. This gets any denial out of my head, and I have to accept it. This is real, and going to school today is going to be torture.

I'm not past the front door of the school when students bombard me.

"How's Jamal doing?"

"How's Jamal's attitude?"

"What does Jamal think he'll do about school?"

"He really can't move his legs?"

Finally someone asks, "How are you doing?" My close friend, Jamal's close friend too, Mia. She is the only mental-medicine I have to get me through the day. The three of us have been friends since kindergarten, and neither Jamal nor I have ever thought of dating her.

We are just like The Three Stooges because we are inseparable and always do funny or silly things, but we have some physical similarities the Stooges didn't have. All three of us have blue eyes. It might be a little unusual for Jamal, but then he has a white mom. We all have dark hair, too.

Mia is like a sister to us. I have always liked her but would be scared to ask her out and mess up the friendship.

"Leave Kev alone! What do you expect him to tell you?" she shouts to a couple of insistent questioners. "Stop bothering him. He can't tell you anything you can't hear on the news." Mia turns to look at me.

"It's not right to ask you all these questions at a time like this. Don't worry, Kev, I will try to stop them from bothering you."

"Thanks, Mia, but you don't have to do this."

Mia smiles at me and says, "I know I don't have to, but I am still going to, and anything you need, just let me know. Well, see you later. I have to get to class."

"Okay, see you later, Mia. Thanks, it means a lot," I say as she scrambles down the hallway.

The bell is ringing, and everyone clears the corridor. Finally I'm alone and it's quiet. I don't even want to go to class, but Jamal would kick my rear if he thought I didn't go.

The rest of the day goes exactly how I expect, with me telling everyone over and over that we don't know if Jamal will walk again. It hurts every time I say it. Anyone who knows Jamal knows if anyone can get back up on his feet, it's Jamal. Saying this out loud helps me feel better.

I can't focus in class this day—all of my teachers can see that.

"If you fall behind, don't worry," Mrs. Robbins, the science teacher, tells me. "We know you'll be spending time at the hospital. If you want, we can send your homework with Mia, and you can turn it in late."

It pays off that I am an A student and a hard worker.

Before I leave to go see Jamal at the hospital, I text Mia. The *whoosh* from my phone lets me know that the message is sent.

Today 4:00 P.M.

I cannot hang out like normal today

Delivered

She texts back.

Today 4:05 P.M.

I get it.
don't worry.
call u later.

Now I'm comfortable to leave for the hospital.

CHAPTER 6

At the hospital, I show Jamal his stack of schoolwork. It's only been a day after he was hit. I really feel lame, but the teachers say it will keep him occupied.

"Put it on my nightstand, please," Jamal commands me.

"The teachers said I can turn this stuff in for you. But there's no hurry, and you can even do some of it online."

As I expect, Jamal has a smile on his face. "Yo, Kev, I already finished some of my work online. Bet you don't have anything done yet."

Of course, he is still the same old Jamal, the hardworking student.

"So how are you doing? What's the plan?" I ask.

"I have to stay here and rest for a week, then I'm transferred to a rehab hospital for a month," Jamal says. "They say there is only a ten-percent chance I will walk again. I told them I will be that ten percent without a doubt, my brother. The doc told me there should be a good amount of recovery within the first six months. That's when I have to work the hardest to walk. After a year, my chances of improving go down. Means I have to work my butt off now, even though I can't feel my butt right now."

I'm afraid the look on my face gives away my feelings. I feel sad he's not able to move when he was just doing 360-degree dunks with ease. But seeing him smile and hearing his optimism makes it impossible for me not to smile back.

I look at him. "So when are we getting started on our *against all odds* challenge?"

He just stares at me for a minute. "Man, you have to do something besides sit here with your brother who can't walk. You need to get a girl while I am stuck in here to help you start with our goal."

I am in shock and have no clue what to say.

"Whoa, wait, what are you talking about?"

Jamal smiles and I can tell he's been doing some serious thinking while he's been stuck flat on his back.

"Mia." He smiles after he says her name.

I know I am blushing and getting butterflies in my stomach.

"What did you say? Did you really say Mia?"

"You heard me. I know she is perfect for you. You guys both act like boyfriend and girlfriend minus all the kissing parts and that stuff already. Dude, you're perfect for her. I know she would say 'yes' and she knows you're too afraid to ask her out."

Oh, he is right. I've had a mini-crush on her for a few years.

"What? Did you guys discuss this?"

"No, I can just tell."

Mia, one of the five coolest girls in the school. Five feet six. My height. And smart. I love her brain.

"We're best friends and get along so perfect. How did you know I like her?"

He looks at me, a little confused. "How would I not know? You always get red whenever you're both sitting close, and you act all stupid around each other. It's obvious!"

"You don't care? Don't you want to take her out?" I ask.

"No, I've got my sights set on a round ball, weighing about twenty ounces, made of rubber, named Spalding. That's my love right now. Speaking of that, when I get out of the hospital, we are working on your game."

"Come on. I'm embarrassed that you guessed my crush on Mia and you also know I really want to be a star. That makes the score two to nothing. You still beat me and you can't even walk right now."

"Kev, you are so easy to read."

"At least let me try to even the score. Let's shoot some baskets here. I'll bring in a plastic hoop to put on the wall and a small ball and we'll have a shootout."

Jamal shakes his head. "Yeah, right, not even in your dreams. I said I would make you the star of the team; I didn't say I would make you better than me."

Since he is right, I just laugh along and say, "All right, I *might* take your advice on Mia, but I'm not giving up on beating you in hospital ball. I'll see you tomorrow."

"Goodbye, sport. I expect you will be playing to Mia and me sitting in the bleachers one day.

You need to ask her out."

CHAPTER 7

I'm visiting Jamal at the hospital, and he is lecturing me.
"Spend more time with Mia!" He doesn't make this as a request; he commands me.

"Okay, okay. Give me a break, will you?" I step into the hospital hallway and take out my phone.

3:25 P.M.

> **hey Mia, let's hang out when leave the hospital.**

Delivered

Mia answers in ten seconds.

> **sure. luv 2**

My palms became sweaty and my knees weak. *What am I so afraid of?* I wonder. *She's like my other best buddy.*

I never had a girlfriend before. I have lots of girl friends, but no one I call my "girlfriend."

Maybe because I am always thinking about Mia whether I am with her or not. It is Jamal, Mia, and me, and we spend most of our time shooting baskets and playing NBA videogames.

I'll do what I usually always do and meet at her house after school.

At least it is a plan. She makes me nervous whenever I am around her. Now I see how Jamal figured this out so well.

I'm not going to mess this up!

After school I go to her house and knock on the front door, and for the first time ever I'm at a loss for words.

"Hey, Kev."

I can feel my face flush. "Uh…hey, Mia. You look really good today."

Mia punches me in the arm and jokes, "What, I look good today? Does that mean I normally don't look good?"

I'm happy she doesn't take it the wrong way.

"Let's head to the park and shoot some baskets, okay?"

Sure, I will follow her anywhere, and the park is a good start.

"So how's Jamal?" she asks. "I stopped to see him yesterday. He either really understands that he's got a tough road ahead or he is just plain delusional."

"He's not delusional. He's probably the most rational person we know, our parents included.

I'm really betting on him coming back and spending time with us, like the old days."

We start shooting baskets, and Mia says, "I feel like you're letting me win. I want you to try your hardest with me."

Embarrassed, I play my hardest game and only win by one. *Wow, if I can barely beat her, how can I replace the best player in the country?*

It's like she reads my mind. "Maybe you should try out for the girls' team this year and I'll try out for the boys'."

The rest of the day we hang out at her house and have dinner there. I love eating with her parents. Her mom is a great cook and makes Chinese special stuff I never get at home. Her parents love me.

"You are such a good influence on Mia," her father says.

"Stop telling him how great he is! He's got to become a lean, mean, basketball machine. He needs some calluses on his personality."

I rarely give Mia a hug goodbye, but this time I make sure to. She backs up and I can tell she is surprised.

"You usually only hug on special occasions. It's not my birthday, is it?"

"No, goofy. I just felt like it."

This time Mia's face reddens and she uses her shy, cute voice. "Bye, Kevin. Today was great.

And I can tell Jamal you're starting to work on your game. Text me later."

"Yeah, today was great and, of course, I'll text you later."

As I walk away I'm thinking, *I know she was blushing and so was I. What can that mean?*

I have a huge smile on my face when I get home. Mom looks at me with a confused face.

"Kevin, you never looked this excited after hanging out with Mia. Something going on between the two of you?"

"C'mon, Mom." I dart for the stairs to get to my room so I can start texting Mia. I call Jamal first. "Hey, man! How you doin'?"

"I'll be out of the hospital in a couple of days and into a rehab place. I could feel my toes a little bit today, though."

"Wow, that's great. You know what else is great?"

"Do tell."

"Mia! She gave me a big hug today. And now I know you had a great day. I'll sleep easy tonight."

And I do. With a smile on my face all night.

CHAPTER 8

Months move on without asking my permission. Suddenly, it seems, it's May. I've been so consumed with Jamal and Mia and school, I pay little attention to time.

I do understand I can't control time or anything besides what I eat. I can't will Jamal better, and that's what I really want to do.

My dad and I drive around at last once a week looking for the white Rav4. I want to ask him to drive by Curtis's house, but it's on the other side of town and I don't want him to think I'm accusing Curtis. I'm really afraid he'll tell me to let the police handle it. That it could be dangerous.

I'll find a way to get him to drive by one day, without his knowing why.

Mia and I seem to be getting closer since it's always just the two of us together. Now every time one of us leaves the other's house, we hug.

With Jamal's improving a little and the doctors saying his chances of walking are getting better, a heavy weight has lifted off my brain. I'm relieved.

The familiar "whoosh" tells me a text is sitting on my phone.

3:15 P.M.

> **get ur skinny butt over here as soon as possible**

It's right after school on a Thursday, and I feel like I've been out of touch with Jamal all day. I have no idea what's going on. I was going to do my homework before I went to see him at the rehab hospital, but he's panicked me. I text him back, but he doesn't answer. I am scared that something bad has happened but also hopeful for good news.

"Mom, I got a text from Jamal telling me to get to the hospital now! Can you give me a ride?" Thoughts are rushing through my head and unfortunately, I always think too much and imagine the worst.

Jumping out of the car at the rehab door, I don't wait for the elevator and run up the stairs to his room. Jamal is perfectly fine and happy to see me like always.

"What's up?" I ask, still trying to catch my breath.

"Take a seat and give me your phone. I need to call someone, and it's important."

I give him my phone and he starts to text someone.

"Man, what are you doing? You're not calling anyone."

Jamal smiles me. "Give me a minute."

I start to go toward him to take my phone when I hear him get a text back.

He hears it, too, and hides the phone. "What, are you really going to fight your crippled brother for a phone over a text or two?"

I have no other choice but to let him keep doing whatever he is up to. I'm thinking of all the things he could possibly be doing that he didn't want me to know about.

Finally, he looks at the new text, smiles, and says, "You're either going to love or hate me for this.

Well, my job for the day is done."

I am terrified of what he's done. I read the texts and realize he's been texting Mia. I am guessing he just needed to talk about a homework assignment.

Why didn't he use his own phone?

I grab the phone from his hand, and before I have a chance to read the texts, he says, "I'm hooking you up, man. Are you going to read the texts or just sit there looking like an idiot?"

5:00 P.M.

> **have you ever thought about being more than friends? we get along so well and Jamal thinks we would be a great couple.**

Delivered

5:23 P.M.

> **Omg...YES!!! I though you'd never ask. I'm so happy and have thought about this for w hile**

5:24 P.M.

> **awesome. a movie tomorrow 2nite?**

Delivered

My nerves are jumping down my throat. I force myself to read the next text.

5:25 P.M.

> **can't wait!! meet at my house around 5 and be ready 4 a fun night**

My jaw drops. I look at Jamal and just can't get words out of my mouth.

He happily jokes. "I told you I had something important. I did this for you. I knew you were too much of a coward. Man, I can help you get your girl, but I can't get you to be great at basketball. That has got to be all you. I can't play for you. Kevin, don't be a chicken, you have to be confident in yourself. Before anyone else believes in you, Kev, you got to believe in yourself. Now, tell me, how long were you going to wait until you asked her on a date?"

I am still in shock at everything he said. "I don't know, maybe a few months...I ..."

Jamal cuts me off and says, "I know you, man, come on. That means you were never going to."

Ashamed, I look at him and just say, "Okay, I admit that I probably never would have."

"Well, now you have yourself a girl. She's beautiful, smart, and fun, and you two are perfect for each other. Mia can help boost your confidence as long as you're not going to let her be the better basketball player."

"I get what you did, Jamal, and all I can say is, thanks. You're truly my best friend and a true brother."

I start to walk out of his room, really sort of floating, and he yells, "Wait! I almost forgot. I know you're not going to do this on your own, so I'm gunna tell you how to kiss her for the first time."

I turn back around to face him. "Yeah, there's no way I was going to kiss her, but if you can think of a way, maybe, sometime, I will. If I can keep myself from getting nervous. So then, tell me, just in case…."

"Okay, now when you're sitting in the movie theater, if you're sitting on her right you have to tell her you see her friend sitting to her left so she looks that way. Then when she turns her head back toward you, put your right hand on her left cheek and lean in and kiss her as she's turning back at you. She'll never expect it, and it will make sure you don't get nervous from having to look at her and then make a move."

Even I'm smiling, but he's laughing.

"Okay, okay, I'll take your expert advice, Mr. Ladies' Man."

"If you mess up, you're doing a hundred pushups the next time you're here!"

CHAPTER 9

I know it's rare not having a girlfriend before your junior year of high school, but all I really ever cared about was basketball. I was never the best and always an underdog because of my height.

But that's what I love about basketball: It's always a challenge to play better than all the people who are taller than me. I love doing things people say I can't do.

Jamal seems to think I can be a star if I ever get a chance. I work harder than anyone else.

People say if I were only six feet tall, I would be a star player, with more talent than anyone on the team besides Jamal. But when the smallest kid on the team—besides me—is five-foot-ten and one hundred seventy pounds, the coaches never want to play me.

Jamal tells me if he had the same height and jumping ability as me, I would be ten times better than him. Well, that may be true, because I am a better version of him, talent-wise, just in a shorter body and no vertical compared to him.

We'd play all year 'round back then for our school in Beverly, always the top team in the area, mostly because of Jamal. Sophomore year and before, I was a star player because no one was too tall compared to me, and size mattered less than skill level then to coaches.

The kids called Jamal and me the most unstoppable guard combo in the area. Some of the other coaches would check Jamal's age because he was always so big and tall and still a guard.

Jamal was great with the pep talks when my height became a killer for me.

"There've been lots of short professional players. You're a point guard, for Pete's sake, the most specialized role of any position. We're like quarterbacks in football. We run the team's offense by controlling the ball and making sure it gets to the right player at the right time."

"I know what we do," I answer back with the most sarcastic voice I can muster.

"Okay, then. You know there've been lots of shorter pros like Earl Boykins from the Houston Rockets. You know how tall he was?"

"Sure, he makes me look tall. Maybe he's five feet four or five inches?"

"Yeah. Five. And he played until 2012. Or how about 'Muggsy' Bogues at five-foot-three inches, the shortest pro player *ever*? He played for the Toronto Raptors."

"Yeah, but that was in the 90s, wasn't it?"

"Okay, I'm pushing this too far, now, right?"

"Right! Dad did do us a favor with the AAU clinics in Boston he sent us to. And the summer camps. It was great."

"Yeah, your dad drove us everywhere to get to those games. It was the bomb. Remember when he started a team in AAU just for us to be on? That's why we have this amazing chemistry together."

"It was always fun because of the rivalries with other towns. The biggest—"

"Yeah, I know. It was with Lynn, the team Curtis played with before he moved to Roxbury."

I only have one more year left to play basketball, but now it's minus Jamal. I'm about to go on my first date. I'm dealing with a lot that should be putting me under a lot of stress, and I'm stretched thin. But thinking about how Jamal is dealing with his situation and how much he believes in me makes me feel great.

CHAPTER 10

I open my eyes and look at my phone to check the time. It's five in the morning and I'm thinking, *I usually sleep 'til seven on school days.* My heart is racing because I cannot stop thinking about my date later, but I am full of that good type of stress—the type I normally get before a big game or test I know I'm going to ace.

School drags on because all I can do is think about the date later. No one but Mia, Jamal, and her friend Jen know about the date. I keep thinking about the way Jamal told me to do the first kiss, and I keep seeing myself messing it up and embarrassing myself. I am going to try it, though, because I feel like it's time. And Jamal will ask, for sure.

When I finally get home, I do a quick workout to calm down. I take a shower and pretend to shave my twelve hairs, which I hate doing, but I never let myself get too much facial hair. It's not like I could grow a beard if I tried.

"Why are you shaving after the gym?" Dad asks.

"Dunno."

Dad keeps reading his book, but Mom smiles at me. I realize I can't change my behavior without them wondering what's up. I figure Mom gets it this time, but Dad seems clueless.

"Well, actually, Jamal told me if I paid more attention to my grooming maybe I could get a girl."

Mom laughs and says, "Kevin, you want a girl? I've never heard you say anything besides that you want to play basketball."

"Yeah, well, Jamal was making fun of me for not having a girlfriend and said that I'll never get one at this rate. You know I love to do things people say I can't do."

Mom shakes her head and walks away laughing.

Around 4:30 P.M. I sneak out of the house and walk to Mia's. She's waiting outside for me with her friend Jen, who's driving us to the movie theater. I get in the car.

"Hi," I say to both of them. I am actually feeling really calm. I look over to see Mia smiling at me. It feels good to be with her.

About halfway there, my phone starts to ring. Mia knew I was going to sneak out and not tell Mom. I freak out and have a mini heart attack.

She sees my panic and says, "Answer the phone, Kev, or she will get suspicious!"

Nervously I answer the phone, and Mom screams, "Where are you?"

I can tell she is scared that I just vanished from the house and didn't say goodbye or where I was going.

I have no idea what to say, and I look to Mia for help and she just shrugs.

"I am hanging out with Brian. He showed up with a few of his friends from out of town and said he wanted me to meet them. They are really cool and love basketball just like me, so don't worry. I am fine. Love you, bye, Mom."

Mom starts to say something, and I just hang up.

Mia smiles at me. "That was close. Glad you're so smart to think fast."

"I don't want Mom finding out we are dating just in case we decide it is better for us to just be great friends."

Then, Jen, in a way that is almost making fun of me, says to Mia, "He is a keeper. It's only your first date, and he is already prepared to even lie to his mom for you."

Mia blushes and gives me a cute smile. I try to hide a smile but can't.

We get to the movie theater and climb out of the car. I look at Mia and notice that she really went all out for the date. She did her hair and makeup, and she looks amazing. Her eyes are so mesmerizing, not even a blue diamond can compare.

We hold hands as we walk into a pizza restaurant. I order a few pieces of pizza, and so does Mia. Mia looks at her food and says she's not hungry. I think to myself, *That's weird that she was just talking about being starving and now she has food and won't eat it.*

I think Jen sees that Mia and I are both nervous, so she does something to lighten up the mood.

She takes Mia's phone and gives it to me. I hide her phone under my seat and show her I have nothing in my hands. She makes Jen and I show her our hands and pockets. Mia goes to check under my seat, and I kick it under the table to Jen. While Mia is looking under the table, Jen passes it back to me. We both laugh.

Mia, somewhat annoyed at this point, says, "What's so funny?"

"Nothing. I just can't believe you lost your phone."

She says, "Oh, yeah, it's so funny, Kevin, so funny. How about we lose yours?"

"How about no?" I say.

Mia gives me a dirty look.

Jen and I play dumb for maybe three minutes, and Mia is getting really pissed because we keep switching who has the phone. She starts looking under random tables, and a cop walks toward her.

"What are you looking for?" he asks.

Of course it's suspicious for a teenage girl to just be looking under random tables, so I run over.

"Sorry, Officer, she was looking for her phone. I found it."

He gives a look of suspicion but just lets us be. Although she's relieved to get her phone back, she gives me a look I know means she will get me back later.

Jen tells us, "I am going shopping while you two lovebirds are at the movies. I'll meet you afterward and drive you home."

There are thirty minutes until the movie starts, so we decide to go in and watch previews. We pick seats at the top in the middle of the theater.

"So this is our first movie together as a couple, not friends," Mia remarks.

Blushing, I say, "Yeah, it is. I'm actually kinda nervous."

"Whew! I thought I was the only one. What a relief. Let's figure out how to calm down. Okay?"

"Sure." I have an idea. "Let's talk about how we got to this point to try to calm our nerves."

"That is a great idea," Mia says. "So, do you remember how we became friends?"

"Of course I do! Me, you, and Jamal all met in elementary school and would play on the same basketball teams in gym class, dominating everyone."

"Right. No one could beat us! It was Jamal and me doing everything, and then you just happened to be in the group. Just kidding. You were good, but we were better than you back then and you know it."

"Fine, I admit it, but I am better then you now."

"Okay, okay, maybe you are better now. But I have a serious question for you."

I get tense because I have no idea what she might ask. "Go ahead and ask anything."

"What finally got you to ask me out?"

Do I tell her the truth? That it was Jamal? Like the story of Cyrano De Bergerac I had to read in English class.

"I just couldn't take not knowing if it would work or not."

She kisses my cheek. "Well, I'm glad you decided that."

The movie she picked out starts. I'm glad she picked *Ice Age: Continental Drift*. If she had picked *The Hunger Games*, it would make me too tense to try to kiss her. This movie is fluff.

We start holding hands, and I feel she wants me to kiss her, but I am too insecure to try. She is staring at me randomly and moving her face really close to mine. I think she is starting to give up hope because she looks a little annoyed, and then stares at the movie. It is time to make my move.

I am sitting on her right, just like Jamal said. I say, "Look over there, I think I see your friend Sarah."

She looks and starts to turn back toward me, saying, "I don't...."

My right hand gently holds her left cheek, and our lips meet and we have our first kiss. The rest of the movie goes great, and we kiss a few times. I have no idea what the movie was about.

Jen meets us outside, and they take me home. I don't feel the ground under my feet.

I kiss Mia goodbye, and Jen whistles. How embarrassing.

Mia texts me right after I get out of the car a block from home.

6:30 P.M.

> **thnx 4 an amazing time.**

My dad winks at me when I get home. It's almost like he can tell I kissed Mia. I'm confused how he could know.

CHAPTER 11

ive in the morning! Why am I up at five in the morning again? Well, whatever the reason, I am full of energy and happy. Jamal will be out of the rehab hospital today, and our training will start soon. Since I am up, I might as well start the day.

Outside the sun is barely up, and not one person is awake in the house. I love training alone, so what should I do? I check my phone and see a text from Jamal from the night before.

9:30 P.M.

> man, tomorrow is the big day. coming home you know what
> that means. the journey starts!!!!!! I made you a schedule.
> make not take 100 Shots
> 100 mid-range shots
> 100 free throws
> run a mile while dribbling a ball
> 15 sprints up and back
> 25 pushups and pulls up.
> have fun bro! (:

Is he kidding? I grab my ball and bag and head out for the local park. I am all alone. The empty court and the basketball in my hands feel like home. A sudden peace always comes over me.

Basketball is my escape from everything and where I feel a lot larger than five-foot-six.

Whenever I need something to cheer me up or to have fun, basketball is there for me. Everything about it has always made me feel good. The feel of the ball in my hand as I dribble, and the control I have over it. The echo of a solid bounce on the ground. Seeing the ball going through the hoop knowing the hard work is paying off.

I love using my brain to outthink another player. Doing a few moves and getting the defender to think I'm going right, then go left, and then either doing a no-look or behind-the-back pass, or scoring after getting by the defender.

That's why Jamal and I have always been good. He was naturally gifted athletically, but what really put us ahead were our minds. We decided the key to success is to always think ahead. Every play, we would look at what was happening and then quickly see a few different options and what could happen from each one, and then make the best play.

The court is my home, my sanctuary, and besides being with Mia now, basketball is the one thing that has been able to help me feel good about myself. Just having a girlfriend has boosted my confidence level a lot, and I feel like a whole new person.

My phone vibrates in my pocket, and I snap out of my thoughts.

6:30 A.M.

---

u better be working hard

I put my phone down to begin my workout. I start with around-the-world, where I make a shot from each dash, the elbows of the free-throw lines, and the free-throw line on the outside of the box.

I keep doing it until I make every shot without missing or I restart. This only takes me two tries.

Then I work on dribbling.

I go up the court forward and return backward as fast as I can, dribbling the ball between my legs with each step. After that, it's dribbling moves with the cones I brought: crossovers, behind-the-backs, be-tween-the-legs, spin moves, and combination moves involving all of them in different ways.

I make the hundred free throws and make an extra ten after that because I always do more than

I am supposed to. I am disappointed because I used to be able to make almost every shot and now I am rusty.

Then the threes begin. I am struggling, so I try to remember the old tips that I had from when I was younger. I need to bend my knees, release the ball at the top of my jump, and hold my follow-through to-ward the right spot until the ball goes in or it hits the rim, and just relax.

I hear a ball go through the hoop on the other side of the park. A familiar voice yells, "What are you doing just standing there? You gave up already, didn't you?"

I turn around to face Mia.

I try to give her a hug, but she says, "No way you're getting a hug, Kev. Jamal told me to make sure you do what you were supposed to. What have you done so far?"

I describe my workout to her.

"I've been watching you the last ten minutes. You have a lot of work to do."

"Well, what do you think I'm out here doing?"

"You're out here being lazy! You're not hustling, you're wasting time and doing everything lackadaisically, and you need to be working harder!"

I hate being called "lazy," but she was right that I was just going through the motions. "Well, are you just going to stand there and tell me I am lazy, or help me out?"

"Come on, Kev. Let's get to work."

We go over to the hoop, and she rebounds for me. My shot is better since I remembered the things my coaches taught me when I was younger.

"Focus!" Mia shouts.

After that, I make a hundred and ten threes.

"Jamal told me all the things he wants you to do. So I know you still have to do more."

"I'm starting my pushups and pullups now."

"Hopefully you don't embarrass yourself; you're supposed to be a strong kid," she teases.

"First I'll do the sprints with the ball and run a mile and a quarter with the ball."

"You better not lose to me, or that's an extra quarter mile."

We walk to the high school track after my sprints.

"Wait, that isn't fair. I'm dribbling a ball, and you're not, so you'll win."

She smiles and says, "You're just going to have to push yourself."

We're four laps through and a quarter mile from finishing, and I am close behind her.

"Bye, Kev!" she shouts, and takes a big lead.

I sprint as fast as I can after her but can't catch up.

I finish the lap and fall to the ground, out of breath.

She walks over and says, "What are you doing? Get up. You have another lap left."

I look at her and say, "Give me a second, I need to catch my breath."

"No, not a chance. You don't have to use the ball this time, just do one more lap. I am starting, and if I beat you on this lap you're doing another."

She starts to run, and I get up and chase her down.

I beat her on the lap, and she says, "Good work, now get some water."

I lie on the ground, mad at myself for losing the first time because I am much faster than her. I am probably one of the top-five fastest people in the whole school.

She says, "Get up, it's time for you to do pushups and pullups."

I walk over to where there is a pullup bar, and I'm about to start when she says, "You won't get a kiss today if you don't impress me on this, or if I don't think you are working hard enough."

I knock out twenty-four pullups. I used to be able to do more than anyone because my dad would punish Jamal and me by making us do pushups, pullups, and crunches. The punishments were not for anything bad, because we weren't bad kids, but more like talking back about chores and not doing chores. I had gotten to two hundred pushups, twenty-four pullups, and two hundred crunches a day by the fifth grade.

I did two more sets and fifty pushups.

"You did okay, but I know you can do better. I'm being nice, though, so you've earned a kiss on the cheek for the day."

I go to collect my cheek kiss, but she yells, "No way I am kissing you! You stink!"

I agree and we go to her house. Her parents know we are dating but agree to keep it from my folks until they figure it out just to see how long it takes them.

We both take showers. She takes one upstairs, and I take one downstairs. After that, we watch a movie and hang out for a few hours, and when I am about to leave, she kisses me on the cheek and says, "That's all you earned today."

"Fine."

I get home and see a huge smile on Jamal's face. I walk over to him and give him a hug, and he hugs me back, giving me a full bear hug, which squeezes all the air out of me. I think that's why he is smiling so big.

"Kev, my arms are getting back to full strength. My legs are still… you know…but the doctor said that it's a really good sign that I have motivation to do my own workout even while doing rehab. Some people give up on the rest of their body when they can't walk."

"I think Mom will be scared of you getting hurt again even though they will be happy you are doing better."

"Both of your parents are really excited. They say the doctors are shocked at how much improvement I am making. Looks like I have a real chance at walking again!"

"Hey, don't think that will make you normal."

He shoots me a disappointed look like I am crazy.

"You're trying to tell me I'm not normal just because I can't walk? I'm still right here, and I'm still the same person. Nothing has changed. I am still the same old Jamal, and if even you, my brother and best friend, can't see that, then I know no one else will."

He is really upset, and I know I messed up.

"I'm sorry. What I said is wrong. You are still all that you were."

"Just go to bed, man, I need to calm down."

Jamal wheels himself into the bedroom my folks set up on the first floor, and I walk up the stairs. I can't believe I messed up like that. I go to bed feeling awful and regret not thinking before I spoke.

CHAPTER 12

Lying in bed that night, I realize the school year had ended, but instead of feeling excitement for summer I just have an eerie feeling. My junior year is over, and I'm the only one in the school not jumping for joy for vacation. I can't celebrate a school year that did what it did to Jamal. Even though Mia and I are a thing, and Jamal and I both finished the school year with almost all A's, I'm not as happy as I should be.

Jamal's feeling better than I am, though. He finished his courses online, and the summer will be full of rehab for him. He did show up to school a few times, but he was embarrassed being in a wheelchair. It bugged him that everyone just stared.

A few of our friends from the basketball team randomly stopped by the house to check in on him. Conversation was stilted, and no one really knew how to talk to Jamal. Typically it was Ben, the team center, and Sam, a power forward, who came to visit. Jamal respected Ben and thought he was the next-smartest player after Jamal and me. Sam was the funniest, but it seemed he lost his sense of humor when he came by. Each one, though, tried to cheer Jamal in their own ways.

Jamal has been happy at home and trying to keep everyone else happy as well. The only time he got upset, besides in school, was when I accidentally implied he is not everything he was before the accident. How stupid was I making a joke about him being in a wheelchair? If I could only suck back those words.

It's been slow progress for Jamal to move his feet. He still cannot move his legs well, but the doctor said any motion is a great sign. Jamal is very excited and optimistic about his future. I am excited for him.

He is also happy for me because of how close Mia and I have become. We are like the perfect combination, and Jamal calls himself the "master matchmaker." And while he is managing my social life, he also manages my workouts. I realize focusing on me lets him focus little less on himself.

"I'm going to surprise you one day soon. I'll be ready to start your training."

I cannot wait for that day.

Mia has told him that I have made progress but thinks I could get a lot better and still work harder. She has been great for me so far. She is there for me if I ever need anything. She's more than a dream come true since she encourages and challenges me on the court. Being a great player herself,

I respect her advice.

I think I love her.

Sometimes she confides heavy stuff to me and I don't always understand. She told me about her grandfather's problems with diabetes. He has rough periods because he doesn't always watch his diet. I've never known anyone else who's ever had the disease. I don't feel I can be helpful, so I try just to listen, not comment.

CHAPTER 13

I wake up screaming from a bucket of ice being poured on my body by my dad.

"What are you doing? Are you crazy?" I'm yelling, and Dad's laughing.

"Jamal said you deserve it, and I don't want to know why, but I enjoyed doing this."

What did I do to deserve this? Trying to remember what I did to upset Jamal isn't easy, and the only thing I come up with is that it's revenge from the night when I got him really upset talking about his not being normal.

"Okay, maybe I do deserve it. So, um, just curious, what time is it?"

"You're not going to believe that I woke up at four this morning to do this to you. It was worth it."

"You cannot be serious.... You're crazy!"

"Crazy or not, time for you to get to work. Jamal is downstairs waiting to go train you. So get up and get to work."

I'm up and when I get downstairs Jamal is all ready to go. If his wheelchair had an engine, it would have been revved up to the highest speed.

"C'mon, Kev, get outside. We have a lot of work to do today. I told you I'd be ready soon to work your sorry rear."

The look of seriousness on face tells me I'm a recruit in his one-person army.

He wheels himself out of the house and down the ramp Dad put together. I have to run to get my stuff and catch up with him.

"Why did you have Dad pour ice on me, and why so early? You still mad I called you 'not normal'?"

"No hard feelings about your recent comments. I got my payback with the ice. You should know that Mom filmed it from your bedroom door and put it on Facebook, and took ten dollars from your wallet because we donated it for you to the ALS Foundation for Lou Gehrig's disease."

"Man, I knew I would be challenged by someone eventually, but at least it gave my family a laugh, not to mention getting Dad out of bed at four in the morning. It's hard to be sore with you."

Jamal is getting a big kick out of my prior ice distress. All of a sudden his face turns serious. "Maybe we can start an ice bucket challenge for spinal paralysis sometime."

"Yes, we can and I'll help all the way. You have lots of friends from everywhere since this happened to you." It's an idea I believe will work and raise money for a great cause.

Once we are in the park, Jamal says, "All right, today is your first real day getting ready to be a star player."

"What are you talking about? I was out here yesterday and did everything you said to do."

He just shakes his head. "Yesterday was the warmup day. Now you are actually going to work hard."

I know he is right. To be the best you have to work harder than anyone. Being short, I am going to have to work twice as hard, but I'm ready for it.

Jamal points to a trashcan off to the side of the court.

"What's with the trashcan?" I ask.

"You're going to be needing that a lot today."

"Sure, man." I'm not going to show him my confusion.

"Trust me. You will see in no time why that's true." He looks me in the eye.

Jamal has me run "up/downs," an exercise that takes me from the baseline to the free-throw line and then back to baseline, then to half court and back to baseline, then to the other free-throw line and back to baseline, and then finally to baseline on the opposite side and back. Every time I run, I have to be dribbling a ball. He starts me at fifty-percent speed, then pushes me to seventy-five percent, and then one hundred percent. After this, he has me start to stretch.

"This is just the beginning of your warmups."

I do fifteen "up/downs" with one ball. I walk over to my bag to get a drink, but he yells, "Get back here! Did I say it was time for a break yet? Man, you a clown."

"Really? I just ran a lot! Can't I have a drink?"

"Look, I would love to be in your situation, but I'm not. You appreciate that you can run, and get back here and run more."

My legs feel like they are burning.

He's right. At least I can do this. I'm lucky to have feeling in my legs, even though it's not a great feeling right now.

Jamal's watch is now my friend. "You have thirty seconds to get a drink, then one minute to stretch out any sore spots."

I hustle to my water bottle to get a few sips and stretch out my quads, which are really tight.

Next, I start shooting. I have to get my own rebound and jog over to get the ball after my first shot goes in.

"Run and get it! Don't jog. Get a workout out of this. I don't want to be here all day watching you be lazy."

I understand and start to run. I shoot thirty-five three-pointers from each spot. I have to make five threes, then fifteen pull-up-off-the-dribble threes. I have to make five dribbling to the right and pulling up, five dribbling to my left and pulling up, and then five dribbling straight. After that I have to hit five doing a step-back dribble to my left and five in a step-back dribble to my right. Finally, I have to hit five more normal threes. I do this from five different spots around the three-point line.

Jamal says, "All right, enough work now, let's head to the track. Catch your breath. Your break is walking there."

I start walking over when a ball is thrown off my back.

You forget something? You are going to dribble this everywhere you go, you hear me, Kev?"

"I hear you, bro, I hear you."

We walk over to the track.

"How many miles do you want me to do?"

"Seven miles."

I look at him and just say, "All right," and start to run.

"Wait up. I didn't tell you what I want you to do yet." I run over to him, and he tells me, "First you're going to do a mile forward, and then a mile backward, dribbling the ball between your legs with each step you take. Then you're doing a mile doing whatever moves you want on the run.

Finally, you're going to sprint five miles."

I get through the first three miles, and then I start to sprint with the ball. Then, as I pass Jamal, I see him waving someone over. The next thing I know, Mia, in running gear, is passing me. I catch up to her, but she just passes me again and takes a full lap lead by the time the first mile is over. I pass Jamal, and he just has a disappointed look.

I think to myself, *I'm going to let it all out. No holding back. Any pain I feel now will eventually be gone. I am going to take the pain now so I feel the payoff later.*

I get myself into an all-out sprint. I know I can catch her. I get within a half lap with three laps left. I am completely out of breath.

I've gotten over the pain and am feeling pretty good that I'm just a quarter lap behind her with a lap left. She looks back and sees me. She looks shocked, and I know I am going to catch her. I'm even to her with a quarter lap left. Dripping with sweat and breathing super heavy, I feel all my muscles aching.

Almost done. The pain will be gone soon. Pain always subsides, but failures do not. I'm shaking my head "yes" to my own inner thoughts.

I sprint ahead of her and get a lead of maybe ten feet. I cross where we had the finish line, and I collapse to the ground.

Mia finishes and yells, "Good work, Kev!" She sees me lying on the ground not moving and screams, "Jamal, Kev's not moving! What do I do?"

"Go check on him, quick."

She runs over to me and sees I'm not breathing.

CHAPTER 14

Mia screams, "He's not breathing!"

Jamal comes over in his wheelchair. "Give him CPR!"

Mia puts her lips on me to start CPR, but I grab her and pull her closer.

"Just needed a kiss to revive me."

She pulls away and slaps me, yelling, "How could you do that to me? You really scared me!"

"Come on, Mia, aren't you happy I'm okay?"

She angrily replies, "Yes, of course, just never do that to me again!"

She hugs me. "I realized from her reaction it wasn't a good prank."

Jamal shakes his head at us. "Pathetic. I guess you earned that for your hard work, but from now on no fooling around. Next up, we're going to the gym."

We head to the gym; today, we're doing weights.

Jamal says, "We are working on your chest and triceps. Mia will appreciate all the work we do with you, Kev."

He laughs, and Mia does an embarrassed but happy smile and says, "Yes, I will!"

Okay, I'm embarrassed but don't say anything.

The person at the front desk laughs and says to Mia and me, "It looks like you both already had yourselves quite a workout."

"They're halfway done, maybe."

The receptionist sees Jamal is talking and instantly looks star-struck.

"Aren't you...you're.... "

Jamal cuts in. "Yes, I'm Jamal Knight."

"Can I have your autograph?" she asks Jamal.

"If you want an autograph, I'll give you one, but I'm just a normal person, especially now." He took our last name when he moved in with us. His original name was Jamal Smith.

She smiles at Jamal. "Here, I have a pen and a piece of paper you can sign."

He signs it, and we continue on as the lady smiles and takes a picture of him.

Jamal looks at me and says, "Time for your warmup. Do as many pushups as you can, then as many dips as you can."

I do as he says, but Mia looks unimpressed with my fifty pushups and twelve dips at a time.

Mia still looks unimpressed.

After that I do eighteen reps with thirty-five pounds on each side, and twelve reps with forty-five pounds on each side, which is one hundred thirty-five pounds, just about what I weigh. I do four other exercises for chest and triceps.

"Good work."

It's great to get a compliment from Jamal, finally.

"Tomorrow we work on shoulders and biceps. Every day you are working on abs and legs, whether it's for conditioning or strength. You need to be bigger, faster, stronger and, most important, smarter than you ever have been. We'll study best players' moves on YouTube."

I smile and try to give him a high-five, but my arms are too sore to lift high enough.

We get to our house, where Jamal wheels himself up the ramp.

He shouts back to me.

"Good work today, Kevin! You shocked me how hard you worked. I'm proud of you, bro. Now you get some free time with our friend."

Wow! Two compliments in five minutes...and in front of Mia.

"Thanks, bro, but I think that you should be the one we are proud of. I mean, really, you are the one who is motivating me."

I can't see his face, only his back as he disappears into the house. I know he is smiling.

Mia and I head for her house.

CHAPTER 15

It's around four in the afternoon when Mia and I walk to her house. She lets go of my hand and moves a few feet from me.

"Hey! What's up? Why did you go all the way over there?"

She covers her nose. "You stink again!"

"Well, you don't smell too good, either, so you can't say anything."

"Fine," she says, and comes back to me and takes my hand.

When we get to her house, I take a shower upstairs and she takes one downstairs. When I come back downstairs, I see her on the couch and she looks beautiful. She has on makeup and nice clothes.

I give her a hug, and she takes off my shirt, smiling, and says, "Mmm, your hard work already seems to be paying off!"

Blushing, I put it back on. "Well, look at you with makeup and dressed nice. I thought you hated being a girly-girl."

She laughs playfully. "Shut up!"

We play another NBA basketball videogame for a bit. She is a worthy challenger, but sometimes I let her win. I don't think she has caught on to my throwing the game sometimes, because she would hate my doing that.

Playing our last game, Mia has the lead with twenty seconds left. She is the Spurs, and I'm the Nets. The videogame is set for the 2013 season and both of my favorite players, Paul Pierce and Kevin Garnett, are playing for the Nets. It kills me they're not with the Celtics anymore, but they are still my favorites. We play this season because I want to play them both on the same team. Pierce has defected to the Wizards now. He's been my favorite player since I was a little kid, so of course I am taking the last shot with him. Mia knows this, and knows exactly what shot is coming. I call an isolation for Pierce, and with ten seconds left I drive toward the basket and hit a patented step-back fade-away elbow-jumper for the game and yell, "You can't handle the truth!"

Laughing, she tells me, "No, you can't handle the truth that I always let you win!"

I know she is kidding, at least I think so, because no one has been able to beat me in this videogame.

By this time it is seven and I'm invited for dinner. We have Mu Shu pork and talk about Jamal, and then how Mia and I are doing. Her parents flatter me, saying things like, "You know, we really like you, Kev," and "We are very happy you're with Mia." This conversation embarrasses me every time.

It's a perfect night. Mia and I decide to go for a walk to the water. I love the Beverly coastline, and she lives close enough to the beach that it only takes two minutes to get there. We grab a couple of towels and snacks and head out. We're really there to be alone and cuddle. The moon is full, and stars light up the sky. I was never as aware as I am now of how beautiful the sky looks. The sparkle of the reflection of the moon on the water is staggering.

Mia looks at me. "Isn't this romantic? We should just lie here all night."

"I know."

Love is grand.

We hold each other for a while, relaxing, looking out at the view. I shift my eyes to Mia's face, and I'm hypnotized.

"Why do you keep staring at me? Look out there! It's an amazing view! How many times can you get a view like this, and a perfect night outside?"

"I'm looking at the most beautiful view I've ever seen. A view I would take over any other."

Her smile shows she loved the comment and that I embarrassed her.

Kissing me, she says, "You really are the best, Kev. I love you."

"I love you, too."

The night goes on, and we have fun with jokes and tickle fights, just enjoying the evening.

Around eleven o'clock, we head back to her house.

"Thanks for an amazing night! I love you. Goodnight," she tells me.

We hug.

This has been the most productive day, and I can't wait to get back and do it again tomorrow.

CHAPTER 16

The summer was too short. Too little time with Jamal coaching me and too little time to spend with Mia alone.

I can't believe I am a senior, because it feels like just yesterday I was a freshman. The thing I still can't believe, though, is that Jamal is in a wheelchair next to me. Everyone in school is used to him being in the wheelchair at this point, and no one treats him differently anymore. That's a good thing. The principal made sure that Jamal, Mia, and I have classes together to keep Jamal feeling comfortable.

It seems lots of people have noticed my body's transformation. I went from a five-foot-six kid weighing only one hundred twenty-five pounds to a five-foot-six kid weighing one hundred forty pounds. I gained fifteen pounds of muscle and now look like a short version of Jamal, physically. I basically have no body fat, just like Jamal used to be.

Mia gets very jealous of the looks I get from some girls and says, "Kev, I see them looking at you. I trust you, and you can trust me. If you break my trust, you better hide or you're going to get the biggest yelling-at in your whole life."

"Mia, you have nothing to worry about. You know me. I would never do anything bad to anyone, especially not the love of my life."

A group of girls walk by and Mia kisses me, right there in the school hallway.

"That'll show them who you belong to."

"I think they know, Mia." This attention is something I'm not used to.

In class the teacher does the attendance. When he gets to my name, he says, "Kevin Knight."

"Here, sir."

"Kevin, do not interrupt me. I was not done speaking yet."

"Sorry, Mr. Alford."

"Okay, as I was saying before I was interrupted, Kevin Knight and Mia Watson are dating." Mr. Alford clears his throat before he goes on. "No girl is to be flirting with Kevin in my classroom besides Mia. As for you, Mia, I will allow some PDA, but not what I saw in the hallway."

The whole class starts laughing except Mia and me, because we are really embarrassed.

Mia says, "I understand, and thank you, Mr. Alford."

The class is still laughing, and Mr. Alford settles them all down.

Throughout the day, people try to talk to us and still ask questions, like how Jamal's recovery is going.

"He's doing great. He's ahead of schedule. If anyone can make it, Jamal is that anyone." I tell this story over and over.

In reality, this isn't true. The doctor told my dad, "I'm frankly worried about his progress.

Jamal should be much further along in his recovery, but he can barely lift his legs. We're going to intensify his rehab. He's not been told any of this because we are worried about crushing his dream of walking again."

Dad told me about the conversation with the doctor. "Push him if you can, Kev. We have to light a fire under him."

After school Jamal either visits a doctor or rehab every day, and most days both. Mia and I feel terrible for him, but there is nothing we can do. He won't let us go with him to his medical meetings.

"Mia, you just keep Kev on point. I'll take care of myself," is his answer to us going with him to rehab.

That's Jamal. Thinking he'll do it and he'll do it alone. Does this have anything to do with his family leaving? I wonder.

Mia and I are extremely close at this point, and everyone says we seem to get along better than any other couples they know.

After school Mia and I say goodbye to Jamal as the medical van picks him up. Now Mia's job is to make sure I'm always at my best. We go to her house and do our homework first. When I try to kiss or hug her, I hear the same words all the time: "No, you have to earn it first." She will randomly kiss me for encouragement sometimes but only on her terms.

"If it looks like you're working hard, you deserve this." Sometimes she teases and fakes as if

I'm going to get a kiss or hug and then says, "Just kidding, keep working, baby." She is in control of our affection times.

We finish our homework and go to the gym. She makes me work hard, and she really loves it, because while she helps me work on my stamina, she's getting herself in shape. We're probably the most fit couple in the whole school.

We usually finish at about seven o'clock and then have an hour together before Jamal is brought back to my house at eight. We look for ways to help him stay upbeat. It seems it isn't so hard; he is upbeat because no one has told him his chances of walking are becoming slimmer.

CHAPTER 17

Basketball tryouts are today, and I feel more ready than ever before. Jamal even admitted that my skills are close to his, except I can't change my height. My five-foot-six to his six-foot-two isn't fair. But Dad says life isn't fair or Jamal would be playing alongside me.

Oh, yeah, a couple of other differences between Jamal and me: There is no way in the world I would be able to get to the fifteen rebounds and five blocks he averaged per game to go along with his solid thirty-five points, ten assists, and three steals.

We may have the best coaches around. Our head coach, Chris Jackson, is a family friend who played Division 3 basketball a few years ago. He is an amazing coach, pushing each one of us to our maximum potential.

I know the whole first day is going to be conditioning to see who stayed in shape over the off-season. The second day we will probably spend working on shooting, dribbling drills, and scrimmaging. Mr. Jackson is a fair coach who will chart our skills and how they translate to the game. No one starts off above anyone; it's all about talent and potential. Seniors who have been on the team for three years can be cut if they didn't practice or stay in shape.

The tryouts are from four until six-thirty at night.

After school, Jamal calls me on his way to rehab. "Hey, man, I need to talk to you."

"You sound serious. What's up?"

"Yo, Kev, it's your first big day. You're ready for this. If you're not, then I have failed you, and

I won't let myself live that one down. Man, you've made me very proud of you."

I'm glad this is a phone conversation and Jamal can't see I have tears in my eyes. I'm choked up hearing his faith in me but also because we are going down two different paths right now. He's not here by my side.

"Well, I have to get off the phone. The van is here. Make sure you warm up and stretch before the tryouts," he says, and then hangs up.

I walk into the gym at three o'clock and start to do some warmups before the tryout starts. The gym is a field house, with one main wood court in the center and a scoreboard over it. It also has a track and two smaller rubber courts, which face sideways to the wood court. For five minutes I've been warming up, and when I go to take a shot, it gets blocked.

"Get that weak stuff out of here!"

I turn around and see Coach smiling at me. He loves soft intimidation. When I was younger, if I wasn't working out at the gym and instead was on my phone or playing with some other distraction, he would pick me up and carry me to the weight room.

The tryouts start with warmup laps and stretching.

Coach says, "Today is the day I am testing to see who is in shape this year. Get on the baseline, grab a ball, and start doing sprints."

We run for an hour and a half until a few kids throw up. I'm feeling good.

Afterward, Coach comes over to me and says, "Wow, look at you. Devin is going to have to work hard to keep up with, today, Kev. Keep up the good work."

"You know I will."

Devin is the starting point guard who, unfortunately, I might have to take the position from, if I earn the spot.

After the tryouts, I walk over to Mia's. A text comes in from Jamal.

7:00 P.M.

u need to come home now! I'm serious u have to home right now!

Mia looks at me. "Well, you read the text. Go home!"

I have never gotten a text like this before, and I am terrified out of my mind.

CHAPTER 18

When I get home, I see our car is gone. I figure my parents are out. Walking in the front door, I see a few of Jamal's basketball trophies are broken and thrown on the floor and that his basketball is popped.

This seems like a horror movie. Jamal is yelling in the background. My heart is racing, and I'm hoping nothing bad has happened to him.

Walking into the living room, I see Jamal looks extremely angry and very depressed. Tears are coming out of his eyes. I am speechless. He holds a picture of himself with the state championship trophy in his hands. I trip over the stuff on the floor, moving to take it away from him before he rips it.

"It's my picture. I get to choose what happens to it. Give it to me now, Kevin!"

"Man, you have to relax. What is going on? You told me to come over here, so I know you know what you are doing is wrong! I'm here now, so please let me help."

Jamal stares at me with tears coming out even more now than when I walked in. He waves for me to come across the room. He falls out of the wheelchair onto the ground.

"I'm sorry, Kev, I just…I just couldn't live in denial forever of what's happened. Look at me, Kevin! I'm in a wheelchair and might not ever walk again. You have no idea what it's like to not be able to walk. It's torture! Especially when the doctors keep saying that I will be able to soon, but I don't feel like I'm making much progr—"

I cut his sentence off midstream. "Hey, don't give up hope, you can get through this."

"Man, I ain't anything anymore. I was going to be in the NBA, man, the NBA. I had everything going for me. Now I have nothing! I'm just some kid in a wheelchair everyone feels bad for. They pity me because I was on top and now I'm nothing. It's torture, every second, just to see how easily people walk around. How they don't have to think about taking one step at a time." He hangs his head and takes a long, deep breath before continuing

"And not being able to play basketball anymore. I just want to play one more time, man, that's all I want. This is not fair! What did I ever do to deserve this? I worked my butt off, have always tried to be a good person, and all I get is a family who can't support me. Then I lose the thing I built my life around, which is basketball. Life isn't fair! I have nothing, man, if I can't ever play again. My whole future was set up ahead of me! We were going to be rich, and I was going to be living my dream. I hate my life now! Why am I even here?"

I get right up in face and start to yell at him. "Man, you're smarter than this! Your life is not over. You have a great future ahead of you, and now you actually have a better chance of helping people, now that you're not going to be playing ball. Sure, you might have made millions and been able to help people with that money, but now you're going to be able to use that gifted mind of yours to help people, in whatever career you choose." I am really getting worked up.

"Your story is inspiring. You need to tell your story of going from a future NBA star, to someone who lost his dream, to a man who is helping people every day with his brain, who is always motivated and working hard to get his ability to walk back. What you achieve and who you are will inspire all those who are paralyzed. You could have been completely paralyzed or died that night! Be grateful for the fact that you *may* walk again. Remember when we talked about an ALS Challenge for those with spinal paralysis?" I push further.

"Man, I could have given up on my dream, but you were pushing me to be better this summer. I kept going because you inspired me to keep going."

I can see Jamal is letting this sink in. He has a small smile on his face now.

"Maybe you're right. Maybe I have had all this happen for a reason. Like, if this never happened, I never would've gotten you to ever ask out Mia, or do any of the work you did this summer."

"Well, that's the light side of what I was thinking," I tell him.

"I see that I can still do good, even with my condition. Thank you, bro, I really needed that. I knew you would save me from all the negative stuff running inside my head. I am not going to let you down, man. You have tried so hard to keep your side of our pact of beating the odds, and I will not give up. You still have a lot of work left to do, and so do I."

"Yeah, dude, we got this. Now we need to keep up the good work. This is just a bump in the road."

We do a handshake, and he says, "Against all odds. The odds are one to one that we'll win. We're both going to do this."

Dad walks into the middle of this emotional moment. He looks at the popped ball and broken trophies on the floor. With a nod of understanding and a sense the storm has passed, Dad says, "Hey, boys, pick up the mess and get ready for dinner."

We both nod.

After dinner I text Mia.

9:00 P.M.

> Jamal lost it today. broken trophies on the floor and a popped basketball. i'm surprised it took him this long to get emotional. he's ok now. we need to spend more time with him.

Mia is optimistic that Jamal will stay positive and do great things, and so am I. Tomorrow is another day of tryouts, and I'm ready to prove myself as a player, not just as someone who is in shape.

I sleep soundly.

CHAPTER 19

It is Day 2 of my tryouts.

And Day 1 of Jamal realizing his new potential.

I eat a huge breakfast and get ready to leave for school. Jamal sits across the kitchen table from me and smiles.

"I'm on a mission. I need to stop thinking about myself all the time and think about how I can use my brain to benefit others. You are right, Kev. Life is beginning again for me."

"What do you think you want to do?"

"I'm not sure, but I know my grades have to be the best for a scholarship to college, where my options can be endless."

"I'm not so selfless as you today. I, on the other hand, am looking to be the best I can be at tryouts today. I think I have more talent than Devin now. He is a bigger kid, so he always got court time in high school. Now it is my time to take over that spot finally. I am not going to let the moment go. I have a chance at my goal, and I am not going to let it slip."

The school day ends with a text from Jamal while I'm with Mia.

4:00 P.M.

> going to spend xtra time in rehab. c u latr.
> u helped me feel better. Thnx

"You did a good thing for Jamal, even though I'm not sure what happened. He seems motivated and optimistic again."

"I'm getting ready for tryouts; I'll tell you about it later."

"All right, go kick some butt out there today."

I go to the park and shoot baskets for a while to stay active and focused. I can feel inside my body that I'm ready for this. The alarm on my phone goes off. It's three forty-five, so I head off to tryouts. The coach is happy to see me.

"So, you ready to show me that you're as good a basketball player as I think you are?"

"Yeah, Coach, just watch."

Coach gathers everyone around and says, "Today is the skills day of tryouts. I get to see how all of your individual skills are. Then tomorrow I get to see who can translate those skills to game situations. There may be players who do not have the best skills but thrive in games because of their knowledge of the game, too." He continues. "You are going to line up into groups based on your positions. Guards, forwards, and centers all go to different spots with different coaches. I'll be with the guards, and we'll go over to the wood court and practice dribbling."

We're doing all the drills I've been doing all summer. My dribbling is great, thanks to Jamal's workout and work ethics he created for me.

Devin doesn't even do as well as expected to be a third-string point guard. When no one is looking, Coach gives me a nod of approval on how I did on the drills.

We move on to passing drills. We use the bull's-eye targets Coach has set up. He also has us make passes to people cutting to the basket and full-court passes. We practice bounce, chest, overhead, behind-the-back, one-hand, football-style, and no-look passes. Devin and I match each other on these.

70

Next, we move on to the shooting drills. Coach has us all take one hundred shots and tallies how many we make from each spot. We need to make a minimum of ten midrange shots, free throws, set shot threes, and off-the-dribble shots.

Devin goes first. He really does not have a good shot at all, because he scores by getting to the rim and making layups or getting fouled. First, he does fifteen midrange, going five for fifteen. He then goes three for ten off shots on the dribble, five for ten on set shot threes, and forty-two for sixty-five from free-throw range. He does almost all free throws because it's the shot he will be taking the most as a point guard. Point guards are always fouled on layups. He is five-foot-eleven and a bit overweight but still fast.

I'm up. I decide that I am going to do twenty-five of each shot to show that I am equally confident in everything. I start with free throws and make twenty-four out of twenty-five.

Then I go twenty for twenty-five on both midrange shots and off-the-dribble shots, but when I make my first twenty threes, everyone at the tryout starts watching to see if I can make twenty-five in a row.

I resolve that my next five threes are going to be from five feet beyond the three-point line. I make all five and the whole group starts clapping, except Devin. Coach gives him a look, and he starts to slowly clap and looks away. I can tell he feels bad about being outplayed, but he should have practiced more.

"Well, look what happens when you work hard and practice. So far Kevin is a model example of how good you can get with hard work." Coach slaps me on the back and walks away.

The tryout ends, and I stay and shoot for a bit.

Coach walks over and says, "Wow, Kevin, you're finally looking like the player we always knew you could be if you ever actually got serious."

"Well, I hope you like what you see, because this is the new me. I'm here to stay."

"I would love for you to stay like this. None of this will amount to anything if you can't do it in a game, though. We both know that. We need someone to spark us now that Jamal is out."

"I know, Coach. I'm not going to let anyone down."

I go home and find that Jamal is still not there and will not be for a bit. Lying on the couch, I think about all the work we did last summer. Jamal and Mia rooting me on. *I'm close to my goal, and all that hard work is paying off.*

I also know I should have been equally focused on working with Jamal. If I had been, maybe he wouldn't have hit the low point.

I'm going to put him first, I think. In reality my goal is just about a sport, and his is about his future. I know that his task is more important. I am not going to let him fail.

CHAPTER 20

It is eleven at night when my phone wakes me up. It's Jamal calling me.

"Hey, man, sorry if I woke you up, but can you come visit me down at the park?"

"Sure, of course. Just give me a few minutes to get ready and get down there."

Jamal hangs up, and I wonder what's going on. When I reach the park, I see him in his wheelchair with a basketball in his hand, shooting at one of the hoops.

"Hey, man, thanks for coming out here."

"What's going on? Why did you have me come out here?"

Jamal shoots the ball, and it goes in. I pick up the rebound, and he signals me to give it back to him. He makes the basket again.

"Man...Kev. You have no idea how much I miss this. It has been so long since I have been able to play basketball, it hurts. It was my life." Looking depressed, he starts to talk again, saying,

"Why, Kevin? Why does this stuff always happen to me? I really just do not understand what I could have done to deserve this."

"Man, I don't know why things like this happen to you. I do know that it seems that the strongest of people have the hardest battles to fight. There is no battle I can see that you cannot handle. I—"

He cuts me off and says, "I realize I am a strong person and can handle it, but why would that mean I have to go through these things? Life isn't fair. The person who hit me with the car got away with it with no consequences."

"Hey, I know life isn't fair. Yes, it is true that the person who hit you did not get caught, but there is nothing you can do about it. Worrying or thinking about things like that is wasted time you could be doing something fun or productive. Yo, man, you know it is true that after every dark night there is a bright day. Bad things do happen in life and you have had some things worse than others, but you can choose to rise from the pain and become stronger from it."

He waves me over and gives me a hug. I know he's trying not to cry. I can see his jaw quivering, trying to hold it back. I'm hoping he won't cry, because when he does cry I feel utterly useless.

"Bro, thank you so much. That does help a lot." His crying does start. "I miss my parents. I don't talk about it, but there is a real hole in my heart. Do you think they don't love me? Are they okay? Where did they go? Why did they not want me?"

I hold him and feel his body trembling as he is crying.

The tears flow down his face like water rushes down a waterfall. I feel his heart racing against me.

I whisper in his ear, "Jamal, I know your parents love you. They gave you up because they wanted to give you a better life than they could give you. So your talents wouldn't be wasted. Your parents wanted to keep you; I know it in my heart. They did this for you. The door to a life with them may have been shut, but they opened the door for you to have a life with my family. We are your second family. When you are eighteen, we can do a search and see if we can find them. It would be better if you were accepted to college before you search. That way, they'll know they did the right thing."

Jamal has stopped crying and is just holding on to our hug.

"I know another door was shut on you with basketball. Maybe that door was supposed to close. Maybe you are meant to be more than be a basketball player. You have a gifted mind, and now you also have a passion about studying paralysis. Maybe this is supposed to be the path you need to go down. You could save lives and help so many people with the research you could do. You could also be an inspiration with your willingness to always get back up after getting knocked down. You can make something out of your life. Who knows, maybe you can also be a basketball coach one day at any level you choose, or work with underprivileged kids, or create a league for people to play wheel-chair basketball."

"I am blessed to have you as my brother, I truly am. Thank you so much, my man. You're right.

I really could make a difference in a lot of lives—"

I cut him off. "I know your parents would be proud of you if they'd heard of what you've been through. We'll tell them when we find them."

"Would you really help me find them?"

"Of course I would. You are family. I will do anything for you, just like you would for me.

Family isn't about blood. It is about those who would do anything to see you smile and who are there for you no matter what."

"True that, homie, true that."

Jamal and I head home. He is quiet the whole way, and I see he is deep in thought about what I said.

I really hope this helped him. Seeing such a positive and mentally tough person cry like that is scary and proves no one is unbreakable; even the mightiest stone can crumble. However, I learned that once you break, it doesn't have to be an irreparable Humpty Dumpty break. Jamal can learn how to build a better life.

CHAPTER 21

I wake up and go downstairs to breakfast. Jamal is not there.

"Hey, Dad, where's Jamal? He never skips breakfast."

"Jamal is down at the library studying about paralysis. He wants to know what causes it and how it is treated."

"Wow, I am proud of him. I know he can put whatever he learns to use one day."

Dad nods his head to agree with me.

School goes by fast, and I see Mia afterward.

"We'll able to hang out more now that tryouts are over," I say.

She gives me a disappointed look.

"Yeah, sure. I mean, I guess we will have more time at some point to see each other."

We agree to hang out next Saturday because it could be the last warm day of the year. It is supposed to be fifty-five degrees.

I get to the gym, and everyone seems to be happy with my performance. They all give me a high-five, except Devin. He just ignores me, and it's obvious to everyone it's because he's scared of losing his spot to me.

Coach calls us over.

"Today is all scrimmaging to see our skills in game situations. This is also the final day of tryouts. Give it your all out there, and remember, if you work hard, it always leaves a good impression. We'll be scrimmaging on the main court for the whole tryout. The groups are going to be Kevin and Devin taking turns as point guard, playing in both the starting group and the non-starting group. Besides that, you know your spots. Between Jeremy, Mike, and Todd, decide which two of you are going to be on varsity and who is going to be on junior varsity. I would like to see you a little later today to get some time in so I know who I might call up in case of an injury. Kevin, you have earned it. You start with the starters, and you and Devin will take turns in the group."

In my group, I have Jordan as shooting guard. He is a great shooter who can also rebound, even at his position. I also have Brian at small forward, a great all-around player who can do just about everything at an above-average level but who does not stand out in any one thing. Sam, a freak athlete, is a good defender but sporadic on how he does offensively. Long and lanky Ben at center is the anchor of our defense.

The other group has Devin at point and Dylan, who led the team in threes last year, as shooting guard. Nick will be a potential X factor this year, because he is a tenth grader who is an amazing scorer but inexperienced at small forward. In this scrimmage, he will be power forward because of his height. Bruno, who is actually a small forward and who can lock down a defender with no offense but his great speed, and Lee, the center who is a solid all-around big man but who needs to develop more, round out Devin's team.

Ben wins the tip, and Jordan passes me the ball. The second I pass half court, Devin is right up in my face and bodying me.

"I'm the starter, and I'm getting this spot back. You're not getting anything easy."

I don't respond, and unfortunately for him the last thing he should have done is get on me so far from the basket. All the muscle I gained in the off-season does not let him body me much. Since I'm the lightest player on the team, I'm also fastest and the quickest. I do a quick hesitation move into a crossover and go right by him. Once I'm by, I'm too fast to catch. I drive down the middle of the court, and after I cross the free-throw line, Lee, who is covering Sam, comes to guard me, and I lob up a no-look alley-oop pass to Sam.

I pick up Devin right off the inbounds and force him to fight for every second up the court. He tries to body me and hip checks me out of frustration. The next play I bring up the ball and run a pick-and-roll with Ben and get another assist. Next, I steal the ball from Devin, and on the fast break he chases me down. I do an up-fake and he jumps by, so I get an open layup.

The rest of the tryout is the same. Devin never gets a chance in the starting group. The one who does is Nick, who shows he is capable of what we hoped and is a very skilled scorer. He is six-foot-one and plays small forward. He is only one hundred sixty pounds but is one level lower than I am at every skill. The only issue is that he has only been playing basketball for a few years, so he is very inexperienced but has great potential. With the rate is he developing as a player, he should be the best player on the team next year.

At the end of tryouts, Coach has a list of the projected roster. It lists the starters and then the role of each bench player off the bench.

1st Game Starters
PG- Kevin
SG- Jordan
SF- Brian
PF- Sam
C- Ben

Reserves
Devin- 6th man
Nick- X Factor/Scorer
Dylan- Shooter
Bruno- Scrappy Defender
Lee- Rebound/Shot Blocker
Mike- Rebound
Jeremy- Play Smart
Todd- JV call 1st call up (if needed)

I know my hard work has paid off, and I can't wait to tell Jamal. I do feel a little bad that I took the spot Devin would have had, but it was never his spot. It used to be Jamal's, and it's my reward for working so hard.

Coach calls us over to pick jersey numbers. I get the fifth pick in jerseys because I am the newest starter. I choose number zero since this is what was expected of me this season. I was supposed to be a zero on the stat sheet, have zero impact on games, and have zero people talking about my playing. No one takes number twenty-three or even thinks about taking it since that number belongs to Jamal and Michael Jordan.

As we leave the tryout, everyone is talking about our first game, coming up in a week. We're playing Lynn, who came in second in our conference last year.

I text Mia.

7:00 P.M.

> **I made varsity. what can we do to celebrate**

Delivered

7:05 P.M.

> **Wow! so proud of you. share a pizza?**

Heading home, I plan on trying to trick Jamal and my parents into thinking I did not make it to see if they really believed I would make it.

I get home while my parents and Jamal are having dinner. When I walk in, they all stop and look at me.

"Well, how did tryouts go?"

Dad is anxious. I can tell because he's blinking fast.

I pause and look upset for a few seconds. "I don't really want to talk about it."

Mom says, "Sweetie, just tell us. We are proud of however you did at tryouts."

I look down at the ground. "Can I just have my dinner and not talk about it?"

My parents agree, but Jamal gives me a confused look.

Right as we are starting to eat, Dad gets a call from Coach. He gives a disappointed look, and the call ends.

How could he be disappointed? Coach must have told him that I got the starting spot.

"I'm sorry, Kev. I can't believe he cut you. He said he appreciates your effort but thinks you are better off focusing on school."

My heart is racing. What is Dad talking about? I am the starter for the first game. He walks over and gives me a hug.

I get really stressed out and yell, "What are you talking about, Dad? I'm the starter for the first game next week!"

Dad, Mom, and Jamal all start laughing because Coach called before I got home and they knew the truth and turned the table on me.

"We're very proud of you. Coach told me he is proud, too, and expects big things from you this year," Dad tells me through his giggles.

"Okay, you got me good. But thanks, Dad."

Jamal yells, "There you go, bro! I knew you had it in you! And you're in my spot. You better do me proud."

"Okay, everyone, relax, I haven't done anything yet."

Dinner ends and I go to bed happy, but knowing I have a lot to prove.

CHAPTER 22

Something vibrating wakes me up. I look to my side and see that it is my phone. The numbers say that it's Mia calling and that it's ten in the morning. It's Saturday and I slept in. Mia and I were supposed to have a really busy day together.

I answer the call, and she sounds very excited and says, "Hey, baby! I hope you're ready for our day. I can't wait to see you, and I will be over in a half-hour."

"Yeah, I am ready to go. Come whenever you can. I have to go and fold laundry."

Wow, that was a lame excuse.

"Okay, will be over soon! Be ready!"

I hang up, quickly take a shower, brush my teeth, and get dressed. As soon as I'm dressed, the doorbell rings.

Mom yells up the stairs, "Kevin, your girlfriend is here!"

I talked to Mia last night to tell her I made it, and she reminded me today is our day. I run downstairs while trying to fix my hair with my hands and open the door.

Mia looks at me and starts to laugh.

"Wait, what's so funny? Why are you laughing at me?"

"Kevin, I know you just woke up and weren't ready. You're folding laundry? Give me a break."

I ask, "Wait, how do you know that?"

"Well, one, your hair is a mess. Two, you were supposed to text me when you woke up, and three, your shirt's inside out and your shorts are backward."

Embarrassed, I ask her to give me a minute to fix myself.

"You're fixing the shirt in front of me. The rest you can fix by yourself."

"Fine." I switch my shirt, feeling self-conscious while Mia and Mom look on.

"Okay, you can go get changed into my attractive boyfriend now."

After I *really* get ready, we head off to the car. Dad has given me the car for the day. We decide to just drive around and jam out to music for a bit.

Mia seems a bit upset. "Pull over in the next parking lot. We need to talk."

Normally, when you are in a relationship and someone says those words, it always means something bad is going to be talked about.

I park the car in the lot, and Mia says in an emotionally distressed manner, "Kev, I'm scared.

How are we supposed to make our relationship work? Seriously, we are both going to be extremely busy during basketball season. Between helping Jamal, basketball, and schoolwork, how are we supposed to see each other and stay close?"

"I'm not sure, Mia. I really don't know. We'll have to come up with a plan."

"Well, you better see that I am more important than some dumb sport. You need to make time for me."

"Seriously, you have to do the same. You haven't done anything yourself to make this work any better but complain."

"Are you kidding me? I want this to work more than anything! How can you sit there and do nothing at all! I do all I can—"

"Shut up!" I can't believe I said that. "Listen, if you want us to work, we have to fight for each other, not against each other. We have to support each other on the things we try to achieve. If you really care as much as you say, you will do that."

She is quiet for a minute, clearly thinking over what I said. I lean over the seat and give her a Hug, and she starts to cry.

"I'm sorry for yelling at you. I agree we have to work together and support each other."

We hug for a few minutes and then drive around for a bit.

After a half-hour, we find ourselves at the beach and stop. I've set up a surprise here and hope it will calm us both.

We are walking along the beach when I say, "I think we should go over and sit in the shade for a little while."

We walk toward a shady area with trees.

"I think we should run here."

We race a short distance, and I let her win.

When we get to the spot I've picked, we find a full picnic set up with a note. She picks up the note and reads it. The note reads,

> *"Dear Mia,*
>
> *I love when you smile. Getting to be with you makes going through any struggle worthwhile. I will make you happy no matter what it takes. When I see you, I am free from stressing, and I say thank you for this blessing. You're my best friend, and I am grateful to have you as my girlfriend.*
>
> *Love,*
> *Kevin."*

Mia has a huge smile on her face and runs over and gives me a tight hug.

"You are the perfect boyfriend. You are so romantic."

"Thanks, Mia. This was the last chance I would get to do something like this until spring. It had to be today."

I have to remember to thank Mom for bringing this stuff over, I think.

"You're the sweetest thing ever."

We have our picnic and when it starts to get too cold, we pack it up and head to the car. We go back to her house and play videogames for a little while—basketball games, of course. I have a new favorite team, the Spurs. They play basketball the way it should be played, and I think they're really fun to watch. She is the Thunder, and I win in a close game, even though she may have had fifty points with Durant. I play team basketball like the real Spurs do and win.

After that I grab something out of my bag. When I pull out a DVD of *The Ice Age*, the first movie we went to, Mia freaks out and gets really excited.

"I can't believe you got it! We have to watch it!"

We watch the movie and have a great night talking about fun times we have had together.

"Thank you for a more than amazing day, Kevin. I love you so much. Goodnight."

"I love you too, goodnight, and you're welcome."

We kiss goodnight, and I head home.

I feel great after the date and know that now I have to turn my attention to our first game against Lynn.

CHAPTER 23

Game day. The first game of the season, and I am getting my first ever start. I go downstairs for breakfast to see everyone grinning. There's a lot of optimism at the table.

"Yo, man, I can't wait to see you out there tonight."

"I would have never have gotten here without you, man."

Jamal laughs and says, "Whoa, man, you haven't gotten nowhere yet."

"Yeah, yeah, I know. I'll impress you, trust me."

"Okay, bro, can't wait to see that."

I shovel in breakfast and head off for school.

At school the kids are talking to me about my first start and how they are going to be at the game. School ends and we get on the bus and head off to Lynn for the game.

In the locker room,

Coach starts his pregame talk.

"Okay, everyone, this is a big game today. I know we won the state championship last year, and

I know we can do it again. But we have to face the fact that no one in this league has any respect for our team without Jamal. You're just as good a team, and I believe in you guys. Let's get out there and get a win."

We get together in a huddle and then run out on to the court. We warm up for the game, and then the ref blows the whistle for the game to start. I can't believe this is my first start. I can feel the adrenaline rush flowing through my body.

The announcer introduces all of the team members and when he says, "Kevin Knight," a chill runs down my back. It could be a dream, except I hear Jamal yelling. My folks are too shy to make a lot of noise.

Ben wins the opening tip, and I get the ball. I get past half court, and the trash-talking has already started.

Jeff, the point guard for Lynn, gets right up in my face and says, "What are you supposed be, little man? You guys replacing Jamal with a shrimp? Man, you ain't getting any points. You're going to have zero, just like your jersey number."

I ignore his comments. I pass the ball to Jordan, and then Sam sets a pick for me as I run to the corner. Jordan gets me the ball back, and I hit the three. I pick up Jeff on defense right as he gets the ball. He bodies me and I get moved off but then get right back on him.

"Man, you're more annoying than a mosquito, and the size of one, too! Get off me." Jeff is annoyed he can't dodge me.

I continue to play hard defense. He passes the ball immediately when he crosses half court again and tries to get away from me. I stick to him like super glue and don't let him get open enough to get the ball back. Even with this tight defense, their center, Andre, manages to score on Ben down in the post.

At halftime, the score is thirty-five to thirty, with us in the lead.

"You're doing a great job out there!"

It feels great to hear the pride in Coach's voice.

I have eight points and five assists so far. I've held my guy to just two points and one assist.

Nick seems a little nervous coming off the bench and only has four points, due to refusing to take a wide-open shot or even dribble. Jordan has nine points, all from threes. Devin seems to be trying to force things to impress Coach and has two points and three turnovers.

In the fourth quarter with a minute left, it's a tie game. I have the ball and dribble up the court. Jordan has been on fire today with five threes, so Lynn switches to zone so we can't isolate Sam down low to draw a foul. They do this while risking a three from Jordan or me, who are both shooting lights out. I give Jordan a look and, since they are in a zone, I split the front of the two-three zone. Jordan shifts from the corner to the spot the guy at the top of the zone moves from. I pass him the ball, and he hits a three.

Jeff brings up the ball and passes it to James, their shooting guard. He is more athletic than Jordan and blows right by him. He hits a runner over Ben, who is late on the help defense. There are forty seconds left when Coach calls a timeout.

"Devin, you're in." Coach knows that Devin is a better foul shooter than Brian.

I bring up the ball. We have a play set up to help Jordan or me get an open shot. I pass it to

Devin, who is supposed to choose the better option between the two of us. The play works: Devin drives to the basket, drawing a double team while Sam's pick gets me open. Devin looks at me, and I call for the ball. He decides to get contact and draw the foul. With ten seconds left and a one-point lead, he takes his free throws.

He hits the first one. The second one hits the front rim, then the back rim, and misses to the side. Kevin, their power forward, gets the rebound and passes it to Jeff, who is running down the court. I get down the court before him and, keeping my hands up, don't move to avoid fouling him.

He jumps into me and elbows me in the chest before making the shot. The ref hesitates and then calls a defensive foul, an and-one.

The crowd goes crazy, and all of us go over to the ref to try to argue, but it is pointless. He is not going to change the call. With just a tenth of a second left, he makes the free throw. We inbound the ball, but then the game ends.

Jeff walks by me and says, "Looks like I squished the annoying mosquito. Learn your place as the second-best team in the conference."

I ignore him as we head to the locker room.

We all sit down, and Coach says, "Fortunately for them, we don't play them again, unless it is in the playoffs. I am proud of how you all played out there. This is our first game without Jamal, and we almost beat one of the top-five schools in the state. No one can complain about the call. I know we should have won the game, but the fact is we lost even though we played well. Don't get down that you lost, but see that you had your first time playing together as a new team and you all played well. When you get a little more chemistry and more comfortable in your roles, we will be a threat to any team in the playoffs."

We get into a group huddle and agree to take this as a sign that we are a team to be reckoned with.

When I get home, Jamal and my parents congratulate me on a good game, complaining that the refs ruined the game on the last call. I had a double-double with eighteen points and eleven assists. I feel good about how I played, but know I can be better. Maybe if Devin had given me the ball… but it doesn't matter to keep going over it. We lost this one.

10:00 P.M.

> heard u played great. proud of u. we won our game. I can teach you how to win

Mia cannot be at any of the boys' games because she has games on all of the same days as we do. I text her back.

10:05 P.M.

> congrats on the win baby. We'll win the next one. I know that much

Delivered

I go to bed with only one thought on my mind: I started for the first time without Jamal. The truth is still hard to take that Jamal won't be playing with me. And I know everything could come crashing down any second, like it did to Jamal. I am not going to take any game or practice for granted. There is not one thing in my life that I should take for granted. I need to start appreciating all that I have. I am going to give every ounce of effort I can in all I do because I do not want to look back after something happens, wondering why I did not try harder or why I did not appreciate something I had.

CHAPTER 24

After that first game, the basketball season is full of amazement. We finish the season with only one loss, the first game against Lynn. No one feels bad, since Lynn won the conference with an undefeated season.

But our season does not go smoothly. Devin and I compete for the starting sport, although he was never close to getting it back. He does play well, but the few times we are on the court together his object seems to be to keep the ball from me rather than help the team win.

Since that first game against Lynn, we grow as a team. Everyone finds their role, and we can play spontaneously, without thinking, based on how familiar we are with each other's strategies.

I end the season with an average of seventeen points and three steals a game. I lead the conference with ten and a half assists per game. When I am named to the first conference All Stars team, Jamal, Mia, and my parents flood our house with balloons that have printed slogans like, "GO FOR IT," "YOU DID IT," "NO REST FOR THE WEARY," and "NBA ONWARD."

Some of my other teammates also have great seasons. Ben averages four blocks a game, the most in the conference, and makes the second conference All Stars team. Sam averages a double-double with eleven points and fifteen rebounds a game, leading the conference, and makes the first conference All Stars team. And Jordan is also a first team All Star, averaging sixteen points and eight rebounds a game.

And then there's Nick, who started slow by averaging fewer than ten points in the first four games but who goes on to average twelve points a game for the next four games. During one game, Brian is out with a sore ankle and Coach steps Nick up to start, which gives him the confidence to play at his potential. He finishes the game with thirty points, twelve rebounds, and two blocks. In the final seven games of the season, he averages more than twenty points a game. Brian keeps the starting spot, but Nick gets more minutes and chances to finish games.

Things besides basketball are going well as well. Mia and I are getting along great and are voted king and queen of the senior class. Her team does not make the playoffs, but she is an All Star. Everything is so positive; I am in a positive trance.

My parents are very proud of both Jamal and me. Jamal is offered full academic scholarships to multiple schools and becomes passionate about studying paralysis and helping people like himself. He has some mobility in his legs, but he hasn't yet been able to walk. The doctors say he might be able to walk, but there are no guarantees.

"I don't want to spend the rest of my life looking up from a four-foot level," Jamal says to me one day. "I have found a place in my heart for the wheelchair, but I believe medical science will come up with something else for me in the future. I know there is research into mechanical devices. I've volunteered to be in a clinical trial. Maybe that is the way I can get back to my six-feet-two-inch perch."

"You'll get there, man. You'll get there." It's a noble lie I tell Jamal because he needs the encouragement. And who am I to tell him mechanical devices might not be around for a long time?

Tomorrow is our last game before the state championship, and of course it's against Lynn.

After what happened during our first game, I don't want our season to end with a loss to Lynn.

Roxbury is already in the state championship with Curtis leading his team. He has moved up to the highest-ranked player in the country.

They won every game by fifteen or more points, with Curtis averaging thirty points, ten rebounds, a few blocks, and a few steals a game. Being six-foot-two and one hundred ninety-five pounds, Sam will have a better chance of stopping him than me.

I don't know why I'm thinking about that game now. We still have to beat Lynn before we can play Curtis.

CHAPTER 25

I wake up really hyper and ready for my game tonight. We're playing at the Boston Garden this year, where the Celtics play. They are on a road trip and decided to let the last two games of the high school playoffs be played on their court. It is my dream to be a pro player, but I know that's highly unlikely and this may be my only chance to play on a pro court and on TV.

At breakfast, Jamal and my parents are all excited, maybe as much as I am. Jamal is going to be on the bench as an honorary assistant coach for this game.

"Man, I cannot wait for this game tonight. I am not going easy on you as a coach tonight. One second of being lazy and I am pulling you out of there. Coach said I have just as much power as he does."

I laugh when I answer. "Then you won't have to take me out, because I go hard every second of the game."

"I know you do, bro, but I have to warn you that I'm being serious."

Jamal and I get dropped off at the school to have a short practice. Jamal is allowed to shoot out of his wheelchair, but he doesn't do it often. He told me he feels like it's a consolation prize rather than the accomplishment it is. Today, he looks at me and says, "Give me a ball. I have to do this."

He holds the ball like a parent holds a baby. I see how much he misses the feel of the rubber in his hands. He dribbles the ball on the side of the wheelchair, and a huge smile comes across his face.

"You have no idea how good I feel right now."

He wheels himself over to the nearest hoop and shoots a free throw. It air balls, missing the rim and the backboard, by a few feet. Everyone sees it.

Only Ben looks Jamal in the eye and comments, "It's okay, Jamal. You will be able to shoot out of that chair eventually."

Jamal snaps. "Someone get me a ball. That was just to see if you all thought I wouldn't be able to shoot with a wheelchair."

I get him the ball, and everyone watches as he shoots another and it goes in. Everyone claps for him, and he says, "Rebound for me."

I give it back to him, and he goes on to make eleven in a row.

"The day I can walk again, I am beating you all in one-on-one. I'm in a wheelchair and haven't shot a ball since last year's championship game, and I still shoot better than you guys. Now as your coach for the day, I am telling you to start practice now."

There is a sigh of relief, and we start to practice. Coach shows up and is happy to see us working hard. A half-hour later, we board the bus for the Garden. After disembarking, we are escorted into the Celtics' locker room. I'm in a fog and can't believe that we are really here. Our names have been put on the lockers. We stand in awe, most of us with our mouths open.

Coach reminds us that we're not doing a tour of this place and have a game today. "Still, enjoy it while you are here."

And are we ever enjoying it. We change and head out to the court, and I'm thinking to myself, *This can't be real.*

We start to warm up, and Lynn comes out to warm up on the other side. They added in a high school three-point line to go with the NBA three. I feel like a real NBA player and remind myself to focus. The refs show up, and we head to the benches. There are a couple of thousand people in the stands, easily the most we have played in front of, not to mention all the people watching on TV.

When they announce the names of the players for both teams, it's easily one of the coolest things I have ever experienced. We head out for the tipoff, and Jeff gets right next to me and says, "Guess mosquitos have two lives, because I squished you once and I am going to do it just as easy this time."

"All I know is that at the end of this game, you are going have respect for me, win or lose, because no matter what, you are not getting an easy win, if you win."

Laughing, he says, "Okay, mosquito."

Ben wins the tip, and Brian passes me the ball. I call a play standing a few feet behind the three-point line. Jeff is standing at the high school three-point line, so instead of running the play, I just shoot it, and it goes right in.

Jeff brings up the ball, and I poke it away and get a fast break. He closes in on me, and I do a reverse layup using the rim and backboard to protect myself from getting blocked. Jeff brings it back down and passes it in to their shooting guard, James, who takes a three from NBA range and misses.

I bring it back down the court and run our team's play called "up," which we used to run for Jamal, but this time it's for Sam. We have everyone on the three-point line, and Sam sets a pick for me. The other guard, who happens to be Jordan, sets a pick on the guy who switches to Sam. I do a no-look pass ball over the top of the smaller player. Sam catches the ball midair and, alley-oop, puts it in the hoop. After both of my baskets, and especially this one, the fans who were neutral to our team go crazy.

It's not the first time the underdogs have become the crowd favorite. Lynn calls a timeout and we head over to the bench, pumped up.

Coach says, "You're only up seven, and just a few minutes into a game. It's not over yet. It has barely even started."

We go back out onto the court, and our lead grows to ten nothing.

At the end of the quarter, the score is twenty to five. At halftime, we're beating them forty-two to twelve, and at the end of the third quarter, it is sixty to twenty-five. It could easily be our biggest win of the year. I have twenty-five points at the end of the third quarter, and Jordan has twenty with four threes. Halfway through the third, we start sitting the starters and putting the bench players in.

In the fourth quarter, against our bench, they've cut the lead to twenty-five when Coach puts in Nick. In this group with Devin, Bruno,

Mike, and Lee, he is the only one besides Devin who can create his own offense. Devin brings up the ball and gives it to Nick, who does a spin move around his guy into a pullup jump shot. He makes it. The next time Devin has the ball, he gives it to Nick again. This time he posts up around the free-throw line. Nick does a fade away right over his defender and hits an NBA three-pointer. Our lead is back up to thirty-two, and it's clear Nick is emerging as a star player.

The game ends with the final score reading: "Beverly, 86, Lynn, 54."

After the game, Jeff comes over to me and says, "You're not bad, mosquito. Now go beat Roxbury in the finals. And you're right, you did earn my respect. You kicked butt and didn't brag, you just acted professionally about it."

"Thanks, man."

We all go into the locker room, celebrating and happy, and Coach yells, "Why is everyone celebrating? What do you think you did that's so great?"

Everyone gets really quiet, and then Coach says, "You're a game away from a state championship. You can celebrate when we win that."

"But we just won the game to get to the state championship and kicked that team's rear!" Ben shouts. "It is time to celebrate. Come on, everyone, get pumped up!" He runs around the room and high-fives everyone on the team, and we all start to celebrate again.

By the time we get home, we are still ecstatic. The local TV sports channel is talking about us.

The announcer, Ray, says, "I thought the only team who would have had a chance against Roxbury would have been Lynn. We all thought Beverly was done this year without Jamal Knight, but with his brother, Kevin Knight, and this Nick kid who has come out of nowhere, it seems they may have a fighting chance after all."

A second announcer, Ralph, pushes back. "I just do not see any way they can beat Roxbury.

They have talent, but Curtis Bryant is just too good and the team is just better overall. I see them winning easily against Beverly."

Ray counters, "We'll just have to watch to find out next Saturday.

One more game and anything can and will happen. And now on to news on the Celtics."

With the TV off, we agree that we think we have a chance and think we will win. Mia comes over, and then we all just relax the rest of the day. When I go to bed, all I can be is happy. It's back to living a dream.

CHAPTER 26

It's the day of the championship game. The game is at eight tonight at the Garden, and I can't wait to start moving. I go downstairs for breakfast and find them all eating already.

"Hey, man, I am your coach again today."

"Awesome. So we are definitely winning now."

After breakfast, we go to practice. Coach is showing a game film of Roxbury.

"I have film on all of their players. We'll go over it one by one for an hour and a half, and then we'll practice."

First is the film on Curtis.

"He's a good dribbler, but not at the elite level. His best traits are his size and athleticism. He is bigger, faster, jumps higher, and is stronger than anyone on our team, except for Sam," Coach nods to Sam's smile, "stands a small chance of being a comparable athlete."

Everyone leans over to pat Sam on the back.

Watching Curtis's online videos shows all his good parts. We see him dunking, hitting every shot, and making amazing plays.

"Learn his favorite moves," Coach says. "He likes to do a spin move or fade away to his right and always tries to dunk the ball when going to the basket. He's also a good post player."

"Hey, Coach, I have yet to see him go left one time. I don't think he has a left at all."

"Good catch, Kevin. We'll test that in the game."

Jamal adds, "Yeah, Coach, Kev's right. He has no left. It worked last year when I would overplay his right side and force him left. He still went right but couldn't get off as easy a shot.

Notice his shooting is really sporadic. He has times of hitting four threes in a row, but then he'll miss almost any shot he takes outside of five feet from the basket."

"We are going to try to get him to be an outside shooter, and if he is driving to the basket or down low, whoever is not on a good shooter will double, and we will force him to be a good decision maker." Coach watches us to make sure we get his drift.

Watching film on the rest of the players, we learn that the point guard, Jake, who is five-foot-eleven, is a good shooter and defender but can't pass. Curtis has the ball all the time, and they don't really use anyone as a point guard.

Their shooting guard, Ray, who is also five-foot-eleven, can shoot just as well as Jordan or I and can't be left open. Curtis is the small forward, and Demarcus is at point forward with Kendrick at center. Demarcus is built like Sam but is a few inches shorter and probably fifteen pounds lighter.

His offensive post moves are good, not great, and he is an okay defender. Kendrick is built like Ben but a few inches taller and has real skill on offense or defense. He is a good athlete for his size. He takes up a lot of room around the rim because of his really long wingspan.

After we study their players, we practice. Warming up, we all go over the game plan in our heads. Getting on the bus, we are off to the Garden for the last time.

I stare out of the window, thinking, *This is it. My final basketball game with team members who have grown to be like my brothers. The last time wearing my number zero jersey. All the work I have put in comes down to this one game. My parents were right when they said to enjoy it while it lasts because life goes by in the blink of an eye.*

In the locker room, we are still just as much in awe as the first time. Our names are back on the lockers, and we feel like they've been etched in history.

When we take to the court for warmups, it is impossible not to notice the stadium is full. There are probably close to an even amount of fans for us and Roxbury. There are different fan sections for the teams to avoid any fighting.

The refs tell us to go to the bench, and then they announce players' names.

Coach Chris walks over to the announcer's table and says, "We would also like to recognize Beverly's assistant coach for the game, Jamal Knight."

"Thanks, Coach Chris. The Boston Celtics salute you," the announcer nods toward Jamal, "and wish you the best going forward."

Everyone in the stands, whether from our side or theirs, claps for Jamal as he is shown on the big screen.

Roxbury wins the opening tip, and they give the ball to Curtis. Sam goes to cover him and then backs off. He does not go farther than the free-throw line.

We get a rebound, and I bring up the ball. I pass it to Brian, who is cutting to the basket, and he goes up for a layup and gets it pinned on the backboard.

Curtis gets the ball and beats everyone down the court for a coast-to-coast dunk.

I bring the ball up and pass it to Jordan, who tries to go by his guy but has the ball stolen from him by Ray. Ray brings the ball down the court, passing it to Curtis, who is down low and who does a spin to his right, hitting a fade-away.

I dribble down the court and decide to launch a three from really deep because my guy was standing too far away. I make it.

On the next possession, Roxbury brings the ball down and Jake passes it to Curtis, who does a give-and-go with Ray. He catches an alley-oop; Sam doesn't see it coming. We get the ball back, but it's stolen from Sam. Curtis goes down the court and scores again.

The rest of the first half goes like this, and at halftime the score is forty to twenty-five, Roxbury. We head to the locker room with everyone but Coach, Jamal, and I thinking that we have no chance.

When we get into the locker room, everyone is silent and looking like they have given up.

Coach walks in and just looks at us, not knowing what to say. Jamal wheels himself in front of the team.

"Everyone, look at me and look at each other. I actually mean look at your teammates. When you do that, you're going to see a five-foot-six kid, who weighs only one hundred forty pounds, who made it to a conference All Star. At the beginning of this season, no one in the conference would have believed he could do that. He beat the odds by working hard and being smart."

Jamal goes on.

"Now everyone watching this game is looking at you guys like they used to look at Kevin. He never got off the bench. No one thinks you stand a chance. Everyone out there has written you off, and Roxbury is already acting like they've won this game…..

"Against all odds," Jamal adds, "you can win this game by outworking and outsmarting Roxbury."

"Right." Coach takes back the conversation. "You play like your lives depend on it, because your basketball lives do. Almost all of you are seniors, and this is our last high school game and maybe last real game. I know how it feels to never be able to play again, but at least I went out on top. That is what you want. You want to finish on top, knowing you gave it your all. The tiredness and the pain you feel goes away, but the pain of knowing you should have, could have, or would have never will."

Coach continues. "So you heard what Jamal said. Now let's get this done. Every possession has to be played like it is our last. Every time we have the ball, we need to make the extra pass to get it to the best shot we can. If it's not your favorite shot, don't take it, unless it's needed, so we can have the best chance of getting points every time we have the ball. On defense, we need to play as if the rim was our family and not let them get by you."

Coach and Jamal really stir us up. Everyone starts clapping and getting pumped up, and we huddle up and yell, "Against all odds, we rise!"

We head out onto the court with a newfound confidence. When the third quarter starts, the only change in the lineup is that Nick is starting this half instead of Brian. I bring the ball up the court and pass it to Jordan, who drives by his guy and has a chance to pull up and shoot but instead passes it to Nick in the corner, whose guy had come over to help. My guy goes over to help cover Nick, which leaves me open. Nick passes it to me, and I make the three.

Jake brings up the ball, and I make every one of his steps up the court difficult. He passes it off because he can't get by me. He gives it to Curtis down in the post, who tries to back down Sam, but

Sam holds his ground, forcing him to take a bad shot and miss. Ben gets the rebound, passes it to me, and then I have a fast break with Curtis chasing me down. I go up like I am going to take a layup but do a behind-the-back pass to Sam as Curtis goes for the block. Sam catches it and dunks it.

At the end of the third quarter, the score is sixty to fifty-two, Roxbury. We have made a small comeback in the past quarter. We can see them getting nervous about their disappearing lead.

In the fourth quarter, there's one minute left in the game. It's seventy-five to seventy-two, Roxbury. I have the ball, and I go by my guy and do a fake behind-the-back pass, tricking Kendrick so I can make the layup.

Jake brings up the ball and gives it to Curtis. He drives in, but I run behind him and poke the ball lose. Stealing the ball, I dribble down the court and pass it to an unguarded Nick, who hits an open three. At this point, we have a two-point lead with thirty-five seconds left.

They inbound the ball to Curtis, and he brings the ball up the court. He dribbles around and just waits until Sam backs up, thinking to prevent a drive to the basket. Instead of driving, Curtis takes a really deep three and makes it. He jumps around, celebrating. Coach Chris calls a timeout, and we head over to the bench with twelve seconds left.

We are huddled around Coach, and he says, "We need offense since we are down one, so Dylan and Devin, you are both in for Sam and Ben. We're going to run a play to have Devin with the ball. He'll do a pick-and-roll with Nick, and we'll have three shooters on the outside to kick the ball out to if we can't get it to Nick."

The ball is inbounded to Devin, and he dribbles to half court. The pick comes, and Nick is covered too well to get the pass. I see this, and notice that my guy is not looking at me but watching the ball, so I run behind his back. I am open under the basket. Devin sees me, and he jumps up like he is going to do a floater but instead drops it off to me. I go up for the layup, and Jake, who has noticed me open, hits me from behind. The ball goes off the backboard and hits the inside of the rim. The time on the clock hits zero seconds. The ball rolls around the rim and falls out. It misses, but thanks to Jake's penalty, I have two free throws. There's no time left. We're down by one.

I walk to the free-throw line. This is a make it or break it. I think, *This is what I worked so hard for! Two free throws away from the championship.*

I look around. The stadium is full, and I am the center of interest. I hear a lot of people yelling my name, and then I hear a voice that sounds very familiar.

Jamal is yelling to me. I turn to the bench and see he is trying to stand up like the rest of the audience. He pushes up with his arms but falls back into the chair. I see him again try to do it. He pushes up with his arms. I see how much of a struggle it is by the look on his face. Coach Chris reaches out and gives him a strong arm to lean on. An incomparable joy rushes through my body.

The entire crowd does a standing ovation. Even the other team and the refs start to clap.

After the clapping dies down a little, Jamal shouts, cupping his lips with his hands so I'll hear him, "Man, you are two free throws away from completing your end of our deal and winning a state championship! If I just stood up, you can hit two free throws. That is nothing. You got this, bro!"

A ref taps me on the shoulder and says, "You have to take the free throws."

Everything happens like it is in slow motion. I take the first shot, and it goes in. The ref gives me the ball for the second one. I dribble the ball twice, my good luck move, and shoot the ball. It's taking forever to get to the basket. It goes in! The fans rush the court, and the team runs out to me, and all I can think about is that we did it. Jamal and I both accomplish our side of the deal. More than winning the game, what matters is that Jamal stands up.

Curtis walks across the court and shakes my hand. "Good game. By the way, I've seen you drive by my house many times. We don't own a white Toyota. All you had to do was ask. Basketball is just a game, and we can be friends in real life. Maybe I can help you look for that car."

I'd blamed Curtis for a year without any proof. I am speechless at his good sportsmanship and offer to help.

"Thanks. Catch you," is all I can get out of my mouth.

Curtis walks over to Jamal, and they high-five each other.